PAPA'S RULES

SUE LYNDON
CELESTE JONES

To Dianne
♡ Sue Lyndon

CONTENTS

Published in the United States of America

Sweet Savage Press

Editing by Maggie Ryan

Cover by AllyCat's Creations

Created with Vellum

ABOUT THIS BOOK:

Orphaned and living on the streets of London, life held little hope for Cammie. That is, until Miss Wickersham took her to Talcott House, where the unfortunate are given everything they need...and then some...to become proper little ladies for the papas selected for them by Miss Wickersham.

Ever since her arrival at Talcott House, Cammie has dreamed of the day she would belong to a papa of her very own. A husband to love and protect her for the rest of her days.

Lord Alexander Cavendish has longed for a little girl to spoil and cherish. When Miss Wickersham introduces him to nineteen-year-old Cammie, it's love at first sight. However, he is not one to spare the rod and when Cammie disobeys, he does not hesitate to bare her bottom and impose proper punishment.

In Papa's arms...and bed...Cammie finally experiences the love and safety she has craved. And when Papa takes his bride over his knee for well-deserved discipline, Cammie's body responds in a most unladylike manner.

Despite his words of devotion, Cammie wonders if a

high-born man such as Lord Cavendish can truly be happy with a girl from the streets.

In order to secure his love, she is determined to follow Papa's Rules.

Publisher's Note: *Papa's Rules* is a historical age play romance novel that includes spankings, sexual scenes, medical play, and other naughtiness. If such material offends you, please don't buy this book.

CHAPTER 1

Miss Katrina Wickersham eyed him from across the desk. Her manners, dress and posture bespoke a privileged upbringing, yet somehow Lord Alexander Cavendish felt quite certain that Miss Wickersham rarely engaged in the gossip, intrigues and rivalries which were the preferred entertainments for women of her social set.

Though they had spent less than forty minutes in each other's company, Miss Wickersham's personality was no mystery. From the prim knot of her hair to the shiny point of her boots, Miss Katrina Wickersham was all business.

Quite clearly, she was a woman of purpose.

"It would appear," she said, "as though everything is in order." The corners of her lips turned up in the tiniest of what might pass for a smile. "If you will sign here," she pointed, "here and here," she pointed twice more, flipping the pages back and forth in an efficient and no-nonsense sort of way, which did not surprise him in the least. Before inking his quill, he gazed upon her until she finally looked away. He had no desire to dominate her, but he did wish to ascertain that she was, in fact, human in some way.

He never liked to question his own judgment, and so he attempted to engage Miss Wickersham in conversation to ease his mind before he put ink to paper.

"Can you tell me more about Cammie?" Though his features were composed, as had been drilled into him since childhood, Lord Cavendish's heart struck a rapid pace as the name of his future bride passed his lips.

To his pleasure, Miss Wickersham's countenance softened slightly and she became, he noted, rather pretty, in an austere sort of way.

"Cammie has been under my care for six years. I found her upon the streets of London." Miss Wickersham closed her eyes briefly as though hiding from an unpleasant vision. "A young man purporting to be her brother was dragging her up the stairs of a London town home where he intended to hire her out as a scullery maid. No doubt it was the best the brother could do for her, at least she would have a roof over her head and food on the table." Miss Wickersham paused, collecting her thoughts.

"I knew the family to whom he had promised the girl, a notorious household with a reputation for cruelty and deprivation. The terrified child was screaming and crying and doing everything she could to promise she would behave and be a good girl, but from the looks of both the brother and the sister, it was clear that money for food was the issue and not the unfortunate child's behavior."

Alexander gasped and reared back, appraising the woman across from him with a new sense of intrigue. "Oh, how shocking," he said, involuntarily.

"Yes," Miss Wickersham said, jutting out her chin defiantly and purposely passing her gaze about the opulent room in which they were seated, "not everyone in this life is as fortunate as you, Lord Cavendish." She sniffed the words and his gaze landed on the silver handled letter opener on his desk, wondering how much food that one item might buy for a hungry little girl.

Properly chastened, he asked another question. "How were you able to obtain Cammie from her brother?"

"I am not without my methods of persuasion," Miss Wickersham said. "A wad of bills and the promise of a safe home and secure future for her were enough. I do not doubt that simply the notes would have been sufficient, but I feel it is important to assure family members, when my little charges have them, that the child will be well cared for...forever."

Her green eyes bore into him until he spoke. "I understand," he said, "I have every intention of seeing to Cammie's needs and wants."

"That is my expectation, sir."

~

"MISS WICKERSHAM WOULD LIKE to see you, Cammie," Garland, the bossiest of all the caregivers, said in an impatient tone.

"But I am not done playing," Cammie replied with a pout, straightening the checkerboard in front of her.

Garland gazed down her nose. "You know what happens when you do not obey Miss Wickersham."

That was all the reminder Cammie needed, though she was not happy about it. She was in the middle of playing checkers with her best friend, Hyacinth. "I must go, Cynny," she said, giving Garland a meaningful glare before walking out of the room ahead of the older girl.

"Hard to believe you are nineteen years old, Cammie, given the way you behave sometimes. We'll have none of that attitude around here," Garland said, giving Cammie's backside a firm swat that sent all the young ladies in the social room into a fit of giggles.

"Cammie's in trouble," a couple of them chanted.

Before crossing the threshold, Cammie turned and stuck her tongue out at the lot of them then spun back around and ran smack dab into the not amused form of Miss Wickersham.

Looking up at the woman who was her guardian and caretaker, Cammie found herself on the receiving end of one of Miss Wickersham's well known and roundly feared scowls. "Camellia," she said, hands on hips, "is that any way for a young lady to behave?"

Subdued, Cammie cast her eyes downward. "No, ma'am."

"That is correct," Miss Wickersham said, taking Cammie's hand and leading her down the hall of the manor which housed several dozen young ladies who had been taken in by Miss Wickersham over the years. The two of them arrived at Miss Wickersham's private parlor where tea had been laid out. Cammie's heart sang. When Garland had told her Miss Wickersham wished to see her, she felt certain someone had tattled on her about sneaking a kitten into the older girls' room last night, but clearly that was not the case if the table was filled with sweet cakes, biscuits and cucumber sandwiches.

Minding her manners, Cammie stood by her seat until Miss Wickersham bid her to sit. She crossed her hands over her lap and waited for her hostess to pour the tea, as a well-behaved young lady ought.

"Thank you for inviting me to tea, Miss Wickersham," she said, using her best grown up manners.

"You are welcome, Cammie." Miss Wickersham favored her with a rare smile. "I have some good news for you," Miss Wickersham said as she poured a cup of tea for Cammie and laced it with two spoons of sugar and a hearty dose of milk, just the way Cammie liked it.

"Good news? What? Please, tell me!"

"Now, now, remember your manners, Camellia. Is that the way a proper young lady behaves? Particularly one of *my* young ladies?"

"Nooo," Cammie said, chastened. "I am sorry, Miss Wickersham."

Miss Wickersham put two biscuits and a slice of cake upon a plate and set it in front of Cammie. Her eyes went wide at the bounty of sweets. Usually Miss Wickersham kept her charges on a strict diet and only allowed sugar laden treats on Saturdays, though sometimes she relented and Cook served puddings for girls who had a birthday. Of course, few of the young ladies at Miss Wickersham's actually knew the exact day on which they were born, but Miss Wickersham assigned each a birthdate, usually based upon the day they arrived in her care.

"If you please, Miss Wickersham, what is the good news you have to share with me?"

A satisfied smiled turned up Miss Wickersham's lips as she set her cup in its saucer and placed both upon the linen covered table between them, all the while maintaining ramrod straight posture. "Thank you for asking in such a polite way, Camellia," she said.

Cammie smiled, glad that she had made her teacher happy. Despite her stern demeanor, Cammie knew Miss Wickersham could also be warm and kind. Maybe even loving. All the girls in her care, though they could be mischievous at times, wanted to please Miss Wickersham. Cammie was no exception. She hated to imagine what might have become of her without the intervention of Miss Wickersham.

Every now and then, Cammie remembered what her life

had been like before she came to be one of Miss Wickersham's girls and a shiver of fear ran through her. Life had been unbearably hard and scary. Very scary. She and her brother were alone on the streets of London where kindness seemed not to exist at all, even for a couple of orphans. Her brother, Robert, had tried to care for her, but the task was Herculean and risk lurked around every corner. As she had gotten older, she had tried to help the situation by venturing out from the dark alley where they had a makeshift shelter, but a young girl alone on the streets attracted the wrong sort of attention and Robert had boxed her ears and taken her shoes to ensure she did not venture far from where he left her. She knew he hated to be so strict with her, but he was only a boy himself, trying to provide for the two of them with the few coins he could earn making deliveries for local merchants. Sadly, they were usually merchants from the mills and not grocers. Though Robert occasionally brought her a pretty scrap of fabric, she would have much preferred some bread or an apple.

There was never enough food. She always felt cold due to inadequate clothing, and her brother, though Cammie liked to believe he tried his best, he simply did not have the time or energy to give little Cammie the love she craved.

Sometimes, late at night, Cammie thought about Robert and where he might be now. She loved him, because he was her brother and he had done what he could for her. Even his attempt to hire her out had been well-intentioned. What else could a girl of her circumstances have expected or hoped for? But, she was wholeheartedly grateful to be at Talcott House where she was warm and fed and safe.

Her mind wandered, traveling back to a night from long ago when she was lying in bed awake and Miss Wickersham found her during her nightly bed check.

When Cammie looked up from her pillow and saw Miss Wick-

ersham hovering over her, her stomach did a flip flop. Miss Wickersham did not like it when her little charges did not follow the rules. But, Cammie could not help it that sleep simply would not come that night.

Holding a finger to her lips to indicate the necessity of quiet, Miss Wickersham took Cammie's hand and guided her from the room she shared with Hyacinth, Rosie and Daisy and down the hallway to Miss Wickersham's study.

Miss Wickersham wrapped the chilled girl in a blanket and set her upon the sofa with strict instructions not to move, then left and returned a few minutes later with a mug of warm milk and two of Cook's best biscuits.

While they nibbled on their treats, Miss Wickersham asked Cammie why a little girl who had played all day long and had even been out in the fresh air for a picnic with her friends was not able to sleep.

Cammie took her time chewing a tiny bit of biscuit and studied her teacher. She did not want to upset Miss Wickersham by mentioning her brother, but she also knew it was wrong to lie.

"There are times when I cannot sleep and I think about my brother. I worry that he will find me and make me go with him back to that awful house where I would have to be a servant."

Miss Wickersham's thin brows flickered upward as though she was surprised and just as quickly returned to their rightful place above her eyes. Miss Wickersham preferred everything to be in its rightful place.

Miss Wickersham cleared her throat. "I am sorry that you are unable to sleep. As you know, proper rest is an important part of a young lady's upbringing. It helps her to grow and be healthy. Sleep encourages pretty skin and hair and bright eyes."

Cammie tried not to laugh because Miss Wickersham harped on the value of sleep all the time. No wonder Cammie had been worried about punishment when Miss Wickersham had found her. "Yes, ma'am," she said.

"Perhaps I need to explain things to you better than I did when you arrived. You are older now, so I expect you can understand if I tell you in a more grown up way. Shortly after you came to live with us here at Talcott House, I went to court to be declared your legal guardian. Your brother has no right, no matter what happens, to try to take you away. You are mine. Mine to care for until I find you a proper papa. A papa who will love and care for you for the rest of your life. You need never worry again about being cold or hungry or forced to work for cruel people. Do you understand?"

Mouth agape, realization washed over Cammie. Until then, she had never fully understood the impact of what it meant to be a resident of Talcott House and be one of Miss Wickersham's girls. Never worry about being cold or hungry again. A papa to care for her all her days.

"Yes, Miss Wickersham," she said when she was able to control her emotions sufficiently. "I think I do understand. Thank you."

"I know how difficult your early years were, Cammie. That is why I have made it my mission for all my charges to be given the childhood they never had. Each girl will be cherished and adored for the rest of her life. Would you like that?"

"Oh, yes. Thank you, Miss Wickersham," Cammie said and never had trouble sleeping again.

"Cammie," Miss Wickersham used a stern tone that brought the girl out of her reverie. "Cammie, are you daydreaming again?"

"No, Miss Wickersham," she replied, sitting up straight. "I was just remembering when you told me that I would live here until you found a papa for me and I never needed to worry about being cold or hungry or frightened ever again."

"I remember that conversation," Miss Wickersham said. "I hope you have been happy here at Talcott House."

"Oh, yes, Miss Wickersham. I have been very happy. In fact, I could not imagine a better place on the whole earth," she said spreading her arms wide.

"What about living in a big manor house with your very own papa to love and care for you and be your husband? You would like that, would you not?"

Cammie's heart fluttered and a funny feeling warmed her lower parts. A papa! She had been wanting a papa ever since she came to Talcott House and Miss Wickersham and the other girls explained to her about how every little girl got to have a papa of her very own someday. Papas were special men who would love and care for their little girls, but also be their husbands and help them to make babies of their very own, too. It had sounded like a dream come true to Cammie. She had even accused some of her housemates of making up tales to tease her because she was new. But, she was soon assured by none other than Miss Wickersham that it was all very true. Miss Wickersham worked very hard to find precisely the right papa for each of her girls.

And now Miss Wickersham had a papa just for her. Her heart fell into her shoes. After waiting all this time, what if she did not like her papa? Or what if he did not care for her?

"Cammie," Miss Wickersham said, leaning toward her, "I thought you would be happy at this news, but you do not appear to be so. Do you not appreciate that I have found a papa and selected you out of all my girls to be his bride?"

"Oh, yes, Miss Wickersham, I am exceedingly grateful. But,"—She paused trying to put together all of the confusing thoughts flying through her brain—"I will be sad to leave here. And...what if he does not care for me?"

"Ah, I see why you are worried, but never fear, Miss Wickersham is here. I have met with your new papa and talked with him very extensively about you..."

Cammie gasped and felt her face heat. "Really? What did you say?"

"I told him you were a very well-behaved young lady who is sometimes easily distracted. Is that not correct?"

"Yes," Cammie said with a giggle. Happiness bubbled up inside her, and she thought she might float around the room. A papa!

"Please, tell me all about my new papa. When can I meet him? Is he handsome?" She had always imagined a very handsome papa for herself whenever the girls talked about it. Dark and brooding, but he would smile and cuddle her to his strong chest, because he was the best papa ever. And she would be the very best little girl, ever. She was sure of it.

"His name is Lord Cavendish and when you are married, you will become Lady Cavendish."

Cammie gasped. "A lady!"

"Yes, a real lady."

"Miss Wickersham"—Cammie threw herself into the arms of her teacher—"you have made all my dreams come true. When may I meet him?"

Miss Wickersham pried the girl's arms from around her neck and returned her to her seat. "We will leave in two days' time," she said. "That will give you an opportunity to pack your things, to say good-bye to your friends and —"

"Ohhhh," Cammie cried. "Will I never see Hyacinth or Daisy or Rosie again?"

"Cammie." Miss Wickersham turned strict. "It is rude to interrupt when someone is speaking. If you are to become Lady Cavendish, you must curb your outbursts." She pointed to the corner where a hard wooden stool was perched. "Go to the naughty chair for your impertinence and when you have finished, then we will continue our discussion, but only if you are able to hold your tongue."

"But what about my papa?" Minimally obedient, Cammie stood and made her way to the appointed punishment, but she dragged her feet and kicked the stool once she reached it. "I want to know about my papa!"

Miss Wickersham, always efficient and sparing in her

movements, navigated the short distance between herself and Cammie in record time, taking her firmly by the shoulder and, while holding Cammie at arm's length, rapidly applied three swift swats of a ruler to her backside. "Now, sit and be quiet or you will force me to spank you on the bare. How do you think Lord Cavendish will feel about a bride who arrives with a reddened bottom because she cannot behave herself properly?"

"Oh," Cammie said after Miss Wickersham released her arm. "I apologize, Miss Wickersham," she said softly as she climbed upon the stool. "But, I want to meet my papa sooo badly."

"An apology that includes the word 'but' is no apology at all, as well you have been told, Miss Camellia. I had great hopes for you and Lord Cavendish, but now I must reconsider. Perhaps you need additional lessons before you can be trusted to represent Talcott House amongst society. Once you leave here, your actions will reflect on everyone at Talcott House, and if you misbehave, it will make us all very sad and embarrassed. It might make it more difficult for me to find papas for all the girls here. You do not want to do that, do you?"

"No, Miss Wickersham," she said to the corner, eyes straight ahead, though her vision blurred from the as yet unshed tears forming in her eyes. Miss Wickersham would not really send another girl to be her papa's bride, would she? Cammie's heart weighed heavy in her chest and she clasped her hands together in her lap, her right leg swinging against the leg of the stool. Her bottom stung slightly in the aftermath of Miss Wickersham's firm application of the ruler, and she squirmed a bit on the chair in an effort to alleviate her discomfort.

"Stop moving and be quiet." Miss Wickersham set a book upon Cammie's head, forcing her to keep it level and be still.

"Use this time to think about how to be a proper bride for Lord Cavendish and how to make me proud of you. When your time is up, if you have done as I have instructed, I will tell you all I know about your papa."

Cammie nodded her head, not daring to speak, but she had already forgotten about the book, and it slipped off her head and landed on the floor with a thud. Miss Wickersham retrieved it with an exasperated sigh and returned it to its place atop Cammie's braids.

Staring at the paint on the wall in front of her, Cammie thought about all the other times she had been called into Miss Wickersham's study and placed in the naughty chair. Being a good girl could be so hard sometimes. Her new papa would want her to behave herself and be the best little girl she could, but, she wondered, would she really be able to do it? Plus, she had heard whispers among the girls that papas and their girls shared the same bed. Why would a papa do that unless he wanted to keep an eye on her at all times, just to be sure she did not misbehave? Either she would learn to be a good girl or she would disappoint her papa.

Would her papa punish her for being bad, the way Miss Wickersham and sometimes some of the other staff at Talcott House did?

She got a funny feeling in her down there parts when she thought about her papa giving her a punishment, like a spanking or a scolding. Did he have a naughty chair like Miss Wickersham? An excited shiver ran up her spine. She imagined how he would use his gruff voice when he was upset with his little bride and would look at her down the length of his nose. She felt her toes curling inside her shoes just thinking about it.

Her own papa. She could scarce believe it. All her years at Talcott House she had been told that one day she would have a papa. Every few months one of the older girls would leave to meet her papa and everyone who stayed behind watched the carriage go out the long driveway. Cammie always felt a little jealous of the girl who got a papa, but also a little relieved that she still had time to play with her friends in the gardens and to get hugs and cuddles from Miss Wickersham when she behaved properly and made her happy.

But she had to admit that of late, she had developed yearnings. They were vague and she did not understand what they meant, but she suspected they related to the things that married people did together. The things that some of the girls whispered about when none of the staff at Talcott House were around.

Heated excitement wound through her body. Soon she would know what until then, had only been whispered about.

CHAPTER 2

"A papa?" Hyacinth grabbed Cammie's arm in a painful squeeze. Cammie knew her friend did not mean to cause harm, but her thin fingers were tight. Cammie tried to pry them off as she answered.

"Yes, Miss Wickersham has found a papa for me."

"Who is he? When will you leave?" Hyacinth removed her fingers from Cammie's arm but continued to stare. "Ohh, I wish I had a papa. When will Miss Wickersham find a papa for me?" Hyacinth put her hands on her hips and pouted.

"Now, now." Cammie tugged on Hyacinth's pigtail of golden curls. "I am the one who is getting a papa. You will have your turn soon. I am sure."

"I am sorry," Hyacinth said, looking at her friend with her big blue eyes. "I will miss you. I do not know if I should feel sad or happy."

"Me too!" Cammie squealed then lowered her face and her tone, glancing over her shoulder to make sure no one else heard her raise her voice. Miss Wickersham had some strict rules about young ladies speaking too loudly, and Cammie had no desire to feel the ruler applied to her bottom again so soon, or to serve another stint on the naughty chair. "Is the building on fire?" Miss Wickersham would ask whenever she heard her charges talking in what she considered to be an unladylike pitch. "Because that is the only reason a proper young lady's voice would reach such a volume."

"Tell me everything about him," Hyacinth said, pulling Cammie to the corner of the garden where the young ladies of Talcott House were spending some time getting Miss Wickersham's required daily dose of sunshine and fresh air. While the others ran around playing tag or pushing each other on the swings, Hyacinth and Cammie shared secrets.

"Miss Wickersham says that his name is Lord Cavendish, and once we are married, I will be Lady Cavendish."

"Ohhh," Hyacinth squealed. "A lady! Oh, Cammie there is no one who will make a better lady than you."

"Thank you, Cynny." Cammie squeezed her friend's hand. "I am very nervous. You know I am just a poor girl from a poor family. I do not even know anything about where my family came from. How can I be a proper wife for a lord?"

"Miss Wickersham would never select a papa who would not be just the right man for you. She loves all of us and wants us to be happy with our papas. She tells us all the time."

"I know," Cammie said, staring at her hands as she worried them together at her waist. "B-but, a lady? And, I do not know how to be a proper w-wife." She put her mouth to Hyacinth's ear and whispered, "What about the things that married people do together? The things that no one will ever tell us? Our special gift, that Miss Wickersham always makes us promise to protect and keep safe. I-I still do not know what she is talking about."

"Oh fiddlesticks," Hyacinth said, then covered her mouth with both hands when she realized she had used a naughty word. "You will be a wonderful wife."

"But what about the other part? Cynny, I need to know." Cammie felt panicked, desperate, even. She had no idea how to be a wife. Her own mother had died so long ago she could not even conjure up an image of her, and there was a decided absence of men at Talcott House. Although the sole purpose of Miss Wickersham's establishment was the training of future brides for wealthy, powerful men, specifics had been sorely lacking. This realization weighed heavily on Cammie's diminutive shoulders, and she implored her friend for reassurance. Unfortunately, Hyacinth had no useful information.

"Cammie, I am sorry. I cannot help you. But, it cannot be that difficult or else Miss Wickersham would have made sure we knew all about it, do you not agree? Or perhaps she will tell you before you leave."

Cammie paused for a moment and considered all she had learned in her years at Talcott House: manners and posture, reading and writing, painting and singing. Her education had been more complete than anything she could have ever dreamed of before her arrival. Surely all those hours of preparation would assist her in pleasing Lord Cavendish. The tension in her shoulders eased a bit and optimism crept into her countenance.

"I am going to miss you, Cynny." Cammie's eyes filled with tears and she sniffed them back.

"I will miss you more."

The two girls sat for a few minutes on a bench in the garden, holding hands while gentle tears rolled down their cheeks.

"NURSE LISTER WOULD LIKE you to come with me to her office." It was bossy Garland again, looming over Cammie the next morning as she finished her breakfast. Cammie looked up at Garland, certain that her face conveyed annoyance. She only had another day at Talcott House and she did not wish to spend any of that time with the silly old nurse.

"I do not wish to go," Cammie said, her chin jutting out impertinently. "I have a papa and I do not need to listen to you anymore, so you can take your bossy self back to Nurse Lister and tell her the future Lady Cavendish has no interest in spending time with her today." Cammie turned back to the last of her porridge giving Hyacinth, Daisy and Rosie a smug smile. All of the young ladies at Talcott House had been set a twitter at the news that Cammie had a papa. The whole morning girls had been stopping her and asking questions about her papa and wishing her good luck. Cammie puffed up with pride every time she told the story about how she would soon be a proper lady, married to Lord Cavendish. Her news was met with envious squeals and more than one of the youthful residents of Talcott House had been taken to stand in the corner for her loud and improper noises.

"I will give you one more opportunity to do as you were told." Garland crossed her arms over her ample bosom and shifted her hips to the left. "You had best be out of your seat and on your way to Nurse's office before I count to three. One..."

"Or what?" Cammie said, waggling her head about on her neck with a dangerous amount of pride and conceit. "What are you going to do to me, Garland? I shall soon be Lady Cavendish and you will still be here bossing around young ladies. Hmpfh. Why ought I to do as you say?"

Cammie glanced about her breakfast table at Hyacinth, Rosie and Daisy, expecting all of them to be suitably impressed with her big girl manners and ladylike demeanor. Surely she was destined to be an outstanding lady for her papa, Lord Cavendish. Instead of the admiration she expected, Cammie's tablemates stared at her with wide-eyed wonder and a reasonable amount of shock. Daisy clapped both hands over her mouth and gestured with her eyes to something significant behind Cammie. A shadow fell across the table and Cammie carefully peeked over her shoulder, though before she could even get her head turned that far, a firm hand landed on her shoulder.

"Now," the scratchy voice of Nurse Lister said, "I wonder why Garland is standing in the middle of the breakfast room counting. A group of smart young ladies such as yourselves ought not to need any help with your numbers. Besides, it is not time for lessons yet, is it?"

"N-no," Daisy said against her palms which still covered her lips, though she lowered them to her lap after Rosie elbowed her in the ribs.

"You know"—The nurse's fingers closed over the small bones of Cammie's shoulder—"I do not care to leave my duties at the nurse's office in case there is some sweet girl who needs my help. But, when Garland did not return with Cammie in a timely fashion, I had to abandon my post and come in search of her. What a shame if one of your sisters here at Talcott House has a tummy ache or a cold. You know all the girls here come to me for care and how frightening and upsetting it would be to arrive and find my door closed and locked. You would not want to be the cause of distress for one of your friends, now would you, Cammie?"

Cammie swallowed hard around the dry lump in her throat. "N-no," she managed to squeak out. "I-I was just on my way to see you, Nurse Lister. I am sure you have something important to tell me."

"Oh, believe me, I do." And quick as a wink, Nurse Lister's hand went from grasping Cammie's shoulder to a firm pinch of her earlobe which she then used to guide Cammie from her seat at the breakfast table, out of the room and down the hall. Nervous giggles followed their exit from the eating area.

"Ouch, ouch, ouch." Cammie scampered to keep up with Nurse Lister. "That hurts."

"How fortunate, then, that I am a nurse, do you not agree?" And Nurse Lister gave an extra tug on Cammie's ear and hurried her along the corridor. When they reached her office, Nurse Lister efficiently retrieved her key and unlocked her door single-handedly while continuing to maintain a solid pinch on Cammie's lobe.

Once inside, she relinquished her hold and Cammie rubbed her ear with her palm, though she dared not meet Nurse Lister's gaze.

"I understand you are to be married soon." Nurse Lister pulled out a stack of papers and began scribbling notes upon them.

"Yes," Cammie puffed up. "Miss Wickersham has found a papa for me. Lord Alexander Cavendish."

Nurse Lister glanced up from her paperwork and peered at Cammie over the top of her spectacles. "A lord, you say? Well, now I have heard everything."

Cammie was not exactly sure what the nurse meant by that, but she felt certain it was not a vote of confidence. Still, she refused to be cowed by a nurse whom she would see no more after this day. "Yes," she said, her voice pert, "I will be Lady Cavendish and you will have to call me Your Ladyship when next we meet."

Nurse Lister put her papers aside and focused her attention on Cammie. "Is that so, Miss Cammie?"

"W-well, yes. I believe it is." Cammie squirmed under the sharp eyes of the school nurse.

"And tell me, little miss Lady Cavendish, do you believe that a proper lady would need to be dragged down a hallway in front of a roomful of her friends because she could not obey a request from the school nurse? A request she knew she was obligated to obey?"

"H-how was I to know what you wanted?" She ought not be so flippant with Nurse Lister, but Cammie simply could not stop herself.

Nurse Lister's mouth puckered in surprise, though she quickly clamped her lips closed into a straight line while she appraised her impertinent patient.

"Well, you are about to find out why I wished to see you. Take off your clothes and lay upon the table."

"Wh-what?" Cammie stared up at Nurse Lister. Although she had often visited the nurse's office when she had a tummy ache or needed to have a tooth pulled, she had never stripped off all her clothes. It was unheard of and she took a step back, clutching her pinafore.

"Did you not hear what I said, little Lady Cavendish?"

The nurse's mocking tone raised her ire, but Cammie also knew she had pushed well past the limit of Nurse Lister's patience. "I-I am sorry I did not come right away when Garland arrived for me," Cammie said. "But I had not yet finished my meal, and I did not want to be wasteful of my food."

"Are you certain what you say is true?"

"Oh, yes, I am quite certain. Miss Wickersham detests wastefulness. We have many mouths to feed, she always says." Cammie gave the nurse a tentative smile.

"Hmmm," the nurse said. "As I recall, your plate was empty when I came to the breakfast room."

"Are you certain?" Cammie pressed.

Nurse Lister paused and gazed down her nose at Cammie as though she had difficulty believing what she had heard. Biting her lip, Cammie wondered if she might have pushed too far with the school nurse. An involuntarily quiver raced across her bottom cheeks. She most certainly didn't want to arrive at Lord Cavendish's manor tomorrow with a reddened behind. The very idea was shameful, and Cammie started to regret her recent insolence. She'd heard whispers that married couples saw one another naked, and while that still seemed like an outlandish tale, she supposed she ought not risk the possibility of Lord Cavendish being greeted by a blushing, red-bottomed bride, just in case there was any truth to that scandalous rumor. Her face promptly heated, as she begun to wonder if she would ever see her future husband without clothes, and if he in return might see her unclothed as well. What did men look like naked, anyway? Were they hairy? Did they have muscles in strange places? What did it feel like to kiss a man on the mouth? And what on Earth did a man's privates look like?

Then she realized the nurse was speaking and Cammie had once again allowed her mind to wander, a habit of which Miss Wickersham had never quite broken her. She straightened and focused on what Nurse Lister was saying.

"... aware of Miss Wickersham's edict on not wasting food and I would not have taken you from the table were I not convinced your plate was clean."

"Oh." Cammie stared at her shoes. She sure wished today had been the day she was leaving to start her new life with Lord Cavendish, her papa. At first she had been sad about leaving Talcott House, but at this instant, she wished to be just about anywhere else. Nurse Lister looked none too pleased with her.

"I believe," Nurse Lister said, stepping closer to Cammie, "that I instructed you to remove your clothes and lie upon the table. You are to have a thorough medical exam. Now, would you like to have your temperature taken first or last?"

Cammie gaped at the nurse and made no move to comply with her instructions. Nurse Lister spoke again. "You are going to have your temperature taken and if you do not move quickly, you will find it a most unpleasant experience."

A small squeal escaped from Cammie's mouth. Not the

thermometer! She clutched her hands around her backside. “Bu-but I feel fine.” She forced a bright smile that she hoped the dour nurse would find persuasive.

“I am sure you do. But it is upon Miss Wickersham’s instructions, so it shall be done. We cannot send you off to your new papa without assuring him that you are healthy and prepared to be a good wife.”

“Oh, but I am prepared to be a good wife.”

“I certainly hope that when your papa gives you instructions you will be more cooperative than you have been here this morning. If you had not been full of shenanigans and impertinence, you would have been finished with your exam and sent on your way to spend the day with your friends before you leave. Now, however, I believe you will need some additional attention so I can assure Miss Wickersham you are prepared to be a proper wife.”

“Ad-additional attention?” Cammie licked her lips, which had suddenly become dry.

“This is the last time I am going to tell you to strip off your clothes, Cammie. After that, I will handle the matter myself. Now, get to it.”

The nurse towered above her, arms crossed, eyes piercing Cammie over the top of her glasses.

“Are you going to watch me t-take off my clothes?”

“I must keep an eye on you, mustn’t I? You have done nothing this morning to assure me you know how to behave at all. It is as though, despite all of the time and effort Miss Wickersham has put into turning you into a proper little miss, you have forgotten everything and have decided to act like a stubborn, uncooperative mite. Is that the way you repay Miss Wickersham for all her kindness? Has she ever asked anything of you in the years you have been here, other than to obey her rules?”

A weight of guilt fell upon Cammie. Thinking back to

what she could recall of her life before arriving at Talcott House, all she could remember was misery and loneliness. Miss Wickersham had vanquished all of that and given her all a little girl could need to grow up. She had even found a papa for Cammie to take care of her for the rest of her life.

"Cat got your tongue? I expect an answer."

"I am sorry, Nurse Lister. I have not behaved properly today and that is not fair to Miss Wickersham."

"Good. But that does not change the fact that you are going to get a meticulous exam. You have wasted enough of my time this morning." With that, the nurse spun Cammie around and opened the fastenings on her dress, untied her pinafore, and tugged the garments to the floor, nudging Cammie with her knee to indicate that she was to step out of the puddle of clothing.

"Chemise, off." Nurse Lister was no nonsense, but Cammie still had trouble following her instructions.

"My, you are a stubborn one. I wonder if I ought to tell Miss Wickersham how much trouble you are so that she can find another little girl to marry Lord Cavendish. I cannot imagine that he would welcome a bride who is as obstinate and troublesome as you."

"Oh, no, no. I will be a good girl. I promise. I am the only one who can be Lady Cavendish and I will do a good job, just you wait and see."

"Then strip out of that chemise and get on the table." Nurse Lister was beyond exasperated, and she gave Cammie's bottom a hard swat. The thin layer of her chemise was no protection and the nurse continued to swat while Cammie pulled the garment over her head and scampered to the exam table, all the while followed by the determined nurse with the firm hand.

Once Cammie was upon the table, Nurse Lister continued to work out her frustrations on the poor globes of Cammie's bottom. "Ouch, that hurts." Cammie moved from side to side in an attempt to get away from Nurse Lister's swats, but the older woman simply moved her palm to meet the cheeks of Cammie's bottom regardless of how fast she moved on the table. "You can wiggle all you want, naughty little miss, but I will not stop swatting until you hold still, so if you know what is good for you, you will end this silliness at once. I believe we shall take your temperature last, so roll over on your back and be quiet."

Cammie obeyed, turning her naked form over and lying upon the examination table completely bare. She wanted to cover herself, but with only two hands, she did not know whether to shield her breasts or her girlie bits. By the time Cammie made up her mind and made to put her hands over her ninnies, Nurse Lister had sprung into action. To Cammie's utter shock, Nurse Lister gathered up a shaving cup and razor, briskly lathering up the dark curls over her womanhood and removing them with a few efficient strokes of the razor. Before her brain had registered what had just happened, the nurse moved on to her next task.

She pushed Cammie's feet toward her backside. "Do something useful and hold your knees apart."

Nurse Lister leaned toward the opening between Cammie's thighs and peered down, as though studying what she saw. Cammie wrapped her fingers around her kneecaps and fought against the flush that felt like it started in her kitty and moved throughout her entire body. Cammie held her breath and closed her eyes, hoping Nurse Lister would be quick about her business...whatever that might be. Never in a million trillion years had Cammie ever expected that a nurse would want to look at her kitty. Scrunching her eyes closed as tightly as she could, Cammie hummed a tune in her head and tried not to think about what was happening.

That strategy worked fairly well until a cool finger

slipped into Cammie's secret folds. Cammie's eyes flew open and a gasp exploded from her lips. Were it not for the firm hand of Nurse Lister holding her shoulder to the exam table, Cammie would have jackknifed into a sitting position and possibly off the table all together.

Instead, she was forced to lie there and experience something so new and strange and forbidden, yet so tantalizing and delicious she held her breath and waited for the Nurse's exploration to continue. Her pink ninnies got hard and achy and her breasts felt heavy while heat thrummed through her body. Her pulse quickened and she gasped.

"W-what are you doing?" she managed to say between labored, shallow breaths.

Lifting her head as much as she could, Cammie gazed down between her bended knees and her eyes met those of Nurse Lister. Embarrassment coursed through her. No one had ever examined her private parts before. The longer she stared at the nurse, with her legs still spread shamefully wide, the deeper her sense of exposure grew. Why was her kitty becoming so hot and tingly? Feeling chastened and vulnerable, she wished she could just disappear in this moment. She also regretted not obeying Nurse Lister more quickly. Her bottom cheeks felt aflame from the hard swats she'd received for not taking her clothes off and climbing onto the exam table at a pace to satisfy the nurse. Though she wished to close her legs and hide her shame, Cammie didn't dare to move. She didn't want another spanking.

"Do you know where babies come from, Cammie?" While she spoke, the nurse's finger continued to stroke the feather lips of Cammie's kitty. Cammie's knees, which she continued to hold, began to quiver.

"Mamas have babies," Cammie stated simply.

"That is true." Nurse Lister added another finger and slid

them in and out of Cammie's kitty like a piston. "But do you know how the mamas get the babies?"

"From papas," Cammie said, gripping her knees hard in hopes of stemming her reaction to what the nurse was doing to her. A fresh wave of heated pulses unfurled from somewhere deep within her, and her toes curled and her back arched slightly, as if she was being drawn toward the strange but pleasurable sensations the nurse inflicted upon her. Dear God, what was happening to her?

"Oh, look how wet you are. Lord Cavendish will be very pleased." Nurse Lister held her two fingers up. They glistened with moisture. Cammie squirmed on the table. Bereft of the nurse's touch, she was eager for her shameful examination to continue, but didn't dare to actually say as much. It would be too humiliating to say the words, but her body did not seem to mind and her hips bucked toward Nurse Lister's fingers as if acting on their own. She felt as if she were hovering on the precipice of some unknown bliss, and she found herself fighting the temptation to reach between her legs and stroke her own kitty. She doubted the nurse would like it very much if she released her knees and got in the way of her examination though, so she wisely remained still. Well, as still as she could manage. Cammie's hips lurched forward yet again, without any conscious thought on her part.

Nurse Lister glanced down at Cammie's naked lady bits. "My, you are an eager one. Yes, Lord Cavendish will be quite pleased indeed."

"Wh-why will he be pleased? And how do papas give mamas babies?" Short of breath and feeling on edge, Cammie mustered every bit of strength in her reservoir to ask those two vital questions, then she laid back against the table. Her compliance was rewarded when Nurse Lister resumed stroking her wet kitty. *Oh, yes,* she almost uttered, then clamped her lips firmly shut out of renewed shame, but she didn't want the nurse to cease her attentions. Not yet. Something was coming. Cammie felt sure of it, as the aching in her privates deepened and sent more heated tingles throughout her entire body.

"Papas give mamas babies by putting their penis inside the mama's kitty, though vagina is the technical term."

"Sometimes it is called a cunny." Cammie startled from the hazy delirium the nurse's touch caused when she heard Miss Wickersham's voice. Her face heated at the realization the headmistress planned to observe this most intimate and embarrassing examination. Even more humiliating was Cammie's reaction to it. Desperate to rub her palms over her tingly ninnies, she had fought the urge and gripped her knees so hard that she had drawn them nearly to her chest. Just a couple more inches and she would be able to accomplish the task by rubbing her thighs against the aching swell of her bosoms.

"Or a quim," Nurse Lister said, stepping to the side to allow Miss Wickersham a view of the proceedings. "Papas put their hard penises inside their brides and move in and out, just like this until the papa's seed spurts out and into the mama's womb, where a baby is made."

It was nearly too much information for Cammie to comprehend, particularly given her vulnerable and distracted position. Perhaps there was some truth to the salacious whisperings she'd heard from the bigger girls, the rumors she had once thought could not possibly be true.

She wanted to close her eyes, but simply could not. Raising her head, she watched as both women examined her most private places and then discussed her as though she were not in the room. The pulsing between her thighs increased, as if her kitty had a heartbeat of its very own. No, not her kitty. She was to be the wife of a lord, and she ought to use a more grown-up word for her privates. She resolved to think of and refer to her kitty as a quim, or cunny, or vagina from here on out. Thank goodness Nurse Lister and Miss Wickersham had finally told her the proper names, lest she make a fool of herself in front of her new papa.

"I believe Lord Cavendish will be quite pleased with Cammie," Nurse Lister said. "She is exceptionally responsive."

"So I see," Miss Wickersham said, the two women exchanging a glance and a smile. It appeared that Miss Wickersham's cheeks pinkened when Nurse Lister gazed at her intently. Though curious, Cammie had no time or energy to wonder about Miss Wickersham's disposition, she was on the verge of exploding. Her breath came in ragged gasps and she could feel a quiver moving through her cunny.

"Oh, look," Miss Wickersham said, "she is tightening her little bung hole."

"That reminds me," Nurse Lister said, nodding her head toward a tray of supplies. "We might as well take her temperature, since she has everything spread nice and wide for us."

"A grand idea." Miss Wickersham went to the tray and retrieved a thermometer. "And so business-like to take care of both things at once."

"I thought you would appreciate the efficiency of it."

"No, no, no," Cammie wailed.

"Oh yes, yes, yes," Miss Wickersham said and gave Cammie a slap that landed in the area between her quim and her bottom hole. Cammie's head swirled. It seemed every nerve ending in her body was concentrated on that part of her anatomy. Heated coils of pleasure wafted through her veins until she thought she might faint dead away.

While Nurse Lister continued to finger Cammie's cunny, paying particular attention to a newly discovered nub at the top, pinching and tugging until Cammie nearly passed out, Miss Wickersham smoothed a cold salve over Cammie's bottom hole. The unfamiliar sensation made Cammie want to both pull away and push closer.

Oh, what was happening to her?

"We are preparing you to be an obedient and pleasing wife for Lord Cavendish," Miss Wickersham said, and Cammie wondered if she had spoken aloud.

"You had best hurry, Katrina," Nurse Lister said, "I do not believe little Cammie will be able to hold back much longer."

Miss Wickersham pushed the tip of the thermometer into Cammie's rosebud. Cammie gasped with surprise and then bit her lip again in order not to cry out. The thermometer seemed to intrude very far into Cammie's private hole and if that was not bad enough, Miss Wickersham moved it round and round, working the pucker of Cammie's bottom.

A spring, like one she had seen inside a pocket watch, tightened inside Cammie's tummy and kept turning and compressing until, just when Cammie thought the spring would snap and break apart inside her in a million little pieces, a mystifying release came over her. She exploded and felt like she had been shattered and thrown up to the ceiling and then gently floated back down to earth. Her breathing was ragged, but that strange tingly feeling was gone, much to her relief. A deep and dreamy satisfaction hummed through her, and her limbs felt weakened in the aftermath of the blissful detonation. She couldn't have moved in this moment had her life depended on it, and thankfully neither Nurse Lister or Miss Wickersham ordered her to do so.

"I believe Lord Cavendish will be quite satisfied with our little Cammie, do you not agree, Miss Wickersham?"

"Yes, very satisfied indeed."

CHAPTER 3

Lord Alexander Cavendish gazed between the brocade draperies of his bedchamber, down the heavily trafficked street of his London neighborhood, then glanced at the clock on the mantle.

He was impatient as a boy waiting for St. Nicholas, he chided himself. Hardly the demeanor of a proper English lord, from a long standing family of the highest order.

What family there was left, at least. An only child, his parents had both passed away shortly after he reached adulthood. The weight of an earldom dropped upon his shoulders sooner than he had expected. Tenants and local businesses relied upon him to manage his estate properly in order to assure their own livelihoods. It was not all balls and cognac, at least not for him.

He knew it was incumbent upon him to produce an heir and he most certainly did not wish to live out the balance of his days alone. He was a man of passion and kindness. However, he was also a man with certain tastes and desires which were not always welcomed and accepted among polite society. When he came of age, he had spent several seasons making the circuit of the London balls and fetes which were the meeting ground for all of the best families. He was, even he had to admit, a handsome man with a sizeable estate and fortune and was, therefore, a target of many ambitious young ladies and their mothers. He had, for a brief period, believed himself sufficiently taken with one such young woman, Lady Honoria Brown, and had given serious consideration to making an offer of marriage to her.

However, one fateful night when she had misbehaved and he scolded her and put her in the corner, as was his want in a wife, she rebuffed his suggestion in the strongest of terms and stormed from the household.

Not only did she refuse to speak to him again, but she had spread rumors about his depravities far and wide. Surprisingly, that had made him more intriguing to a few young ladies. Regardless, he found none of them appealing and thereafter refused to attend any of the social events which were intended for those seeking spouses. He had grown lonely, and so when he had heard, through a friend with similar interests, about Miss Katrina Wickersham and Talcott House, he contacted her and much to his delight, a proper young miss had been found for him.

Cammie.

He imagined her all smiles and light, with dark curly hair in pigtails or braids. Sitting on his lap and calling him Papa.

The idea of it heated his insides and fired his loins. He had no interest in tampering with a lady who wasn't yet of a marriageable age, he simply wished for a woman, a real woman, who would allow him the honor of caring for her in a fatherly manner which would please them both.

Miss Wickersham's charges had all been street urchins or foundlings. Miss Wickersham appeared to be some sort of social do-gooder, which intrigued him a bit. He had ample assets and status and no need of marrying to improve his income or social standing. What he desired was a little miss to be his wife.

Movement outside the window caught his attention and he hurried to take a peek. A serviceable but not elaborate carriage stood in the driveway, the door opened to reveal first Miss Wickersham's familiar form followed by a delightful little creature who stole his heart in an instant.

Cammie. His little Cammie tripped delicately down the steps of the carriage and looked up at the expanse of Ashton Manor with eyes wide and mouth agape. Alexander stepped away from the window, not wanting to be caught out spying upon his new arrivals, though he continued to observe from above.

She was perfect. A tiny button of a nose, large brown eyes, and a petite, but womanly form. Dressed in a plain but pretty blue gown, which was cinched at the waist and tied with a thick white ribbon, she embodied everything he had hoped for in a bride, and more. His heart filled with affection for his diminutive future wife and he rushed from the room and down the stairs in an uncharacteristic show of enthusiasm.

His butler paused in the hallway and stared at him in surprise. "I beg your pardon, my lord, I have come to relay the arrival of Miss Katrina Wickersham and Miss Cammie Hughes."

Alexander pushed past the servant and down the stairs, though he forced himself to assume a proper demeanor before entering the drawing room to greet his guests. No, only one guest. Cammie was the other half of his soul.

Taking a deep breath, he strode into the drawing room and got his first up close look at little Cammie, the treasure of his heart. His pulse thudded in his ears and he fought against the huge smile that his lips seemed determined to form. There was no point in being so animated as to frighten his bride or her guardian.

"Good afternoon, Miss Wickersham," he said, giving the taller of the two women a slight bow.

In return, she curtsied and reached out her hand to bring Cammie forward. "Good afternoon, Lord Cavendish. May I present to you, Miss Cammie Hughes."

Cammie's large brown eyes gazed up at him and the corners of her pink lips formed a nervous smile. His heart filled with wonder and awe. How had it been possible for Miss Wickersham to find the perfect tiny angel for him?

He took Cammie's hand between both of his and returned her smile. "Welcome, Miss Hughes. I hope that you will not mind if I call you Cammie."

The girl darted a quick glance at Miss Wickersham who gave a barely discernible nod of approval and a relieved smile broke out across the girl's face. "Yes, I would like that."

He continued to hold her hand in his, and drew it to his lips, placing a gentle kiss to the soft fabric on top of her gloved hand. "Welcome to Ashton Manor, Cammie."

He felt her quick inhalation of breath, though his lips had been barred from contacting her flesh, and he glanced up to see her face flush pink, but she did not withdraw from his touch neither did she shy away from his gaze.

Miss Wickersham cleared her throat and Alexander broke contact with Cammie. "I believe there are just a few more matters for us to discuss, Lord Cavendish, and then I shall be on my way and you and Cammie may have some time to become acquainted before I return with the vicar."

"Yes, of course. Shall we go into my library?"

"Cammie," Miss Wickersham said, "we shall be only a few

minutes. Please wait here. Do not leave this room and do not touch anything, do you understand?"

Alexander took a bit of offense at Miss Wickersham giving his little Cammie instructions, but until the final paperwork was completed and Miss Wickersham exited the premises, he supposed it was she and not he who had the final say in Cammie's conduct and care. It would only be a matter of hours before the wedding took place.

As he escorted Miss Wickersham from the room, he glanced over his shoulder at Cammie and gave her a wink. The giggle that escaped her lips danced across his heart.

~

CAMMIE OBEDIENTLY SAT upon the sofa, crossed her ankles and folded her hands in her lap. After the incidents of the day before, particularly the time she spent in the nurse's office, Cammie had been subdued and obedient, but also eager to explore more about the mysteries of the marriage bed. Her interlude on the exam table in Nurse Lister's office had been both humiliating and enlightening. She squeezed her thighs together, forcing pressure on the nubbin which the nurse had taunted with insistence until Cammie had exploded.

Forcing her thoughts away from such lascivious and unladylike musings, she took in her surroundings. Her new home.

My, but the drawing room of Ashton Manor was large. The entire estate made her head spin. When they rode up the bustling street she had practically crawled over Miss Wickersham's lap in order to get a better look out the windows which were on the older woman's side of the carriage. Now Cammie was inside and could scarce believe this was to be her home...forever. Not only would it be her home, but she would be the lady of the house. Lady Cavendish.

Just saying the name, even if only in her mind, made her tummy flip flop. Lord Cavendish was even more handsome than she had dreamed about. He was tall, with dark hair and eyes, but he was not frightening at all. Cammie had been concerned that she might be frightened being with a man all by herself since such things had never been permitted at Talcott House, but now that she had met Lord Cavendish, her papa, and he had smiled and winked at her, all she could think about was crawling up into his lap and snuggling close.

Oh dear. That funny tingly feeling she had in her lady bits the day before...during the humiliating examination at Nurse Lister's office...returned.

Last night, her final one at Talcott House, she had broken a rule and touched herself. Beneath the covers she had replicated Nurse Lister's fingers as they moved in and out of her cunny. The release which enveloped her had not been as strong as the one she'd experienced in the nurse's office, but it was satisfying nonetheless.

Her fingers itched to touch herself again, but such a thing would be scandalous. She ought to do something about it, but she did not know what. Maybe walking. She had been sitting for a very long time, an especially long time for a little girl. There had been the ride in the carriage to Ashton Manor and now she was being ever so patient and waiting for Miss Wickersham and Lord Cavendish to conclude their business.

And then Miss Wickersham would leave and she would be all alone with Lord Cavendish. Oh no. The tingling got stronger, making a heated pulse between her thighs. Maybe if she reached up her dress and underneath her chemise, a few little strokes to her cunny would quell her sudden urges. She bit her bottom lip, considering such impulsive naughtiness, but soon dashed such thoughts away. What if Lord Cavendish and Miss Wickersham returned while she was touching herself? The very idea of anyone, particularly her soon-to-be husband, catching her in the act of pleasuring herself made her go hot with shame.

Cammie jumped up from the sofa and began to circle the room, careful not to touch any of the beautiful objects that filled the space. The last thing she needed at this critical point in her life was to do something to cause Miss Wickersham to call her naughty and take her back with her. If she disappointed Miss Wickersham and had to go back to Talcott House, Cammie knew it would be a long, long, very long time before she got another papa. Maybe not ever. She might end up having to become a caretaker like Garland, mean and cranky and doing errands for Miss Wickersham and the nurse.

A shiver ran up her spine. Cammie would hate being an errand girl.

But, she did miss Hyacinth. The two friends had tried to keep their spirits up when Cammie had said good-bye that morning, but when Cammie saw Hyacinth's lip start to quiver, she could not hold back and soon the two girls were hugging and crying. It was only the promise of a lifetime of love with her new papa that had caused Cammie to let go and say her good-byes. Maybe someday Hyacinth would get a papa and the two girls could spend time together.

Cammie hugged herself around the middle. If only Cynny could meet Lord Cavendish. Cammie could scarce believe that such a handsome man wanted to be her papa and the idea of showing him off to all of her friends at Miss Wickersham's filled her with delicious anticipation, though no other girl had ever brought a papa back to the house. In fact, in all the years she had been there, Cammie could not think of anyone who left and then returned for a visit.

Perhaps it was because they were too busy with their papas.

Gazing through the window, Cammie saw a small garden just outside. There was a terrace with potted plants and right in the very middle was a beautiful hyacinth plant, the exact same shade of blue as her friend's eyes. Though she was ever so excited to arrive at her new home and meet her papa, nervousness made Cammie wish for something familiar, and she was sure the pot of flowers was a sign meant to comfort her. Besides, she could use a distraction to keep her from reaching up her skirts and seeking out her secret nubbin. Breaking that rule would be worse than disobeying Miss Wickersham's edict that she stay put, she reasoned.

Finding the door to the terrace, she opened it quietly, and made sure not to let it close behind her lest it lock. Just one minute to go and touch the flower and smell its sweet perfume was all she needed and then she would be back inside sitting on the sofa just the way she had been when Miss Wickersham and Lord Cavendish had left her. And, hopefully, the fresh air would help her settle enough to resist the temptation of touching her cunny once she came back inside.

She made her way quickly to the collection of flowers and gently touched the edges of the hyacinth. Just thinking about her friend and her home back at Talcott House calmed her nerves. Relieved and feeling better, Cammie turned and hurried toward the door. She was only two steps away when a large cat walked alongside the house, and in its determination to inspect Cammie, it strode past the door and pushed it closed. Cammie gasped and lunged for the door, but she tripped over the cat, fell and tore her dress.

A moan of horror escaped her lips when she looked down and saw the gash in her skirt. Looking closely, she saw not only a tear in her dress, but her stocking as well. Well, her skin was scraped and raw looking, but at least she wasn't bleeding. That brought her a little comfort.

Gathering herself up as best she could, she made her way to the door only to find, as she had feared, that it was locked. She rattled the knob, but no luck.

Oh, she was in trouble for sure. Not only had she disobeyed instructions to stay put, but she had torn her dress and stocking.

Maybe if she could just get back inside she could cover up the damage to her dress and Miss Wickersham and Lord Cavendish would never know the difference. Her primary goal was to get Miss Wickersham off the premises and back with the vicar to perform the marriage as soon as possible before Miss Wickersham had a chance to change her mind and force Cammie to leave with her rather than allowing her to marry Lord Cavendish.

Because force is what she would have to use. Cammie had already decided life at Ashton Manor with Lord Cavendish as her papa was better than anything she ever dreamed of and Miss Wickersham would have to pry her fingers from the door frame before Cammie would leave the premises.

Moving carefully so as not to make any noise or draw attention to herself, Cammie made her way around the large manor house intending to find the front door and let herself back in, then she could return to the drawing room, sit down and wait for Miss Wickersham and Lord Cavendish. She made good progress around the house but stopped abruptly when she glanced in one window and saw Miss Wickersham and Lord Cavendish seated across from each other at a desk. Miss Wickersham's back was to the window and Lord Cavendish was busy looking at papers on his desk. Maybe luck would be with her. She carefully squeezed between the shrubs and the house, praying she did no further damage to her clothing. Only a few more steps before she would be past the windows.

She carefully let out the breath she had been holding and stole one last glance into the room occupied by Miss Wickersham and Lord Cavendish. Miss Wickersham continued to face away from Cammie, but at the very moment she glanced at Lord Cavendish, he looked up from the papers on the desk and their eyes met.

A shiver of heat ran through Cammie and she could feel her pulse hammering at the base of her throat. She froze in place, hoping that if she did not move, he might not really notice her.

Lord Cavendish quickly returned his attention to Miss Wickersham and Cammie continued her quest for the front door.

Perhaps she had imagined the eye contact between herself and Lord Cavendish. It had lasted only a moment.

On shaky legs she made her way back inside and closed the door quietly behind her with a sigh of relief. Thankfully, the drawing room was just steps away, and she entered and resumed her seat, a calm countenance upon her face, with seconds to spare before Miss Wickersham and Lord Cavendish returned. Acting as though nothing was amiss, she greeted them both with a cheerful smile, while holding her breath, waiting to see if Lord Cavendish had indeed seen her outside the window.

She studied the faces of Miss Wickersham and Lord Cavendish for signs that Lord Cavendish…her papa...had noticed her outside the window and further, any indication Miss Wickersham was unhappy or that Cammie's plans to stay at Ashton Manor forever might be thwarted in any way. Miss Wickersham seemed almost girlish in her demeanor toward Lord Cavendish. Cammie had never seen her teacher so animated before, and if she was not mistaken, there might have been a slight flush to Miss Wickersham's cheeks, as though she found Lord Cavendish rather appealing herself.

However, much to Cammie's relief and delight, Lord Cavendish seemed only to have eyes for her. His dark gaze never left her face, except only for the briefest of moments in response to whatever Miss Wickersham had to say. Cammie was flattered by his attention and also pleased to see that he was a gentleman and treated Miss Wickersham properly as well.

He truly was perfect.

Cammie began to relax, particularly when Miss Wickersham, rather than taking a seat, headed toward the doorway. Hopping up from the sofa, but careful to keep the torn side of her dress angled away, Cammie followed the others to the door and bid Miss Wickersham good-bye. Miss Wickersham promised to return in a few hours with the vicar.

She had done it! Miss Wickersham was gone. The vicar would soon arrive and no one was the wiser that she had broken the rules. What a glorious day.

Suddenly an overwhelming force drew her to Lord Cavendish and she turned to look up at the man with whom she would spend the rest of her life. He towered over her, but even without that advantage of height, his mere presence was daunting. His eyes seemed not to miss a thing and Cammie felt as though he could see into her very soul. She smiled up at him, though he did not smile in reply.

Uh oh. Cammie's tummy did a somersault. What had gone wrong?

He took her elbow. "Shall we return to the drawing room, Cammie?"

His touch on her arm sent a heated thrill through her and her breath caught in her throat, making it impossible for her to reply other than to nod. Papa led her to the same sofa where she had been instructed to remain just moments before and they sat down next to each other. Cammie stared at her hands which were folded in her lap. The length of her dress covered her torn stocking and scraped knee, but had he noticed the tear in her dress?

"Cammie," Lord Cavendish said, turning toward her, his face quite serious, "I am glad we have some time alone to talk before we get married. There are some important matters for us to discuss."

"Oh?" was all Cammie could come up with to say. What more could there be? Had not he and Miss Wickersham already covered all of the details? Surely if they had unfinished business, her teacher wouldn't have departed to collect the vicar.

"As your papa, I have certain expectations." His deep tone was mostly kind, but held a hint of scolding that had her lady bits tingling and heating.

"Yes," Cammie said, a blush covering her face. "Nurse Lister explained to me about...about...how babies are made." Her voice trailed off into a nearly imperceptible whisper as she finished her sentence, such an embarrassing topic for their first private conversation.

Lord Cavendish chuckled and some of the seriousness left his face. "I am happy to hear that, Cammie. I ought to have been more clear in what I was saying." He cleared his throat. "Let me start again. I expect obedience in all things, and that includes my wife." His gaze held Cammie's and she felt her heart drop to her toes. "Do you understand?"

"I-I believe so, sir."

"I also expect honesty and truthfulness, and you can rely on me to give the same in return."

"Yes, sir."

"I also believe in punishing those who disobey me."

Cammie sat up straighter and felt the muscles of her bottom clench up. "Punish?"

"Yes, I expect obedience from you and if it is not given, there will be punishment. I want you to understand all of this before we agree to be married. If it is not acceptable to you, or you are unwilling to trust me to provide guidance and discipline when needed, then I believe, much as I hate to say it, it would be best for us to part ways."

Cammie gasped and stared at him. His face was no longer stern, but seemed to have a cast of sadness about it, the same sadness she felt at the prospect of losing him as her papa.

"No," she said. "I do not want us to part ways. I-I understand your expectations and I agree. I need a papa who will take good care of me and make sure I behave properly. I..." she trailed off and stared at her hands again before looking him directly in the eye and saying, "I want you to be my papa, and I want to be your bride, more than I have ever wanted anything in my whole life."

She held her breath, feeling as though her entire world might come crashing down in an instant depending on how he responded. Her vision clouded and her eyes burned, and she blinked hard a few times in an effort to keep herself from crying. The prospect of having to return to Talcott House and never again see the very man she'd believed would be her forever papa filled her with so much sadness, it took all her willpower to keep from bursting into tears.

Lord Cavendish smiled down at her, and his kind expression helped her relax and blink away the burn in her eyes. As he continued smiling, her heart danced around in her chest.

"Thank you, Cammie. I am pleased to hear that." He paused for a moment, as if carefully considering his next words. "Now," he finally continued, his manner becoming stern again, "can you explain to me why I saw you outside my window just a few minutes ago after Miss Wickersham clearly told you not to move from your place on this very sofa?"

Cammie felt the color drain from her face. It was on the tip of her tongue to deny his statement, but his words about truth and honesty rung in her ears and she wisely chose to acknowledge her misdeeds.

Wringing her hands together, she spoke. "I-I was nervous and I felt lonely and a little bit scared and when I looked outside, I saw a flower that reminded me of my best friend, Hyacinth, and so I went outside...just for a minute...to smell it and touch it. It made me feel much better and I only meant to be outside for a minute, but then a big cat came by and walked right past the door and it closed and locked before I could get to it." She paused and snuck a glance up at him. His face gave no hint of what he was thinking. "So, you see, I had to get back in the house and that is why I was outside your window. I am very, very sorry. Please do not send me back with Miss Wickersham. I promise to be a good girl always."

"Cammie," he said, gathering her hands in his, "I am not going to send you back with Miss Wickersham simply because you were naughty. I do, however, intend to impress upon you the importance of wifely obedience. I regret that I must punish you on the day we are to be married, but I will not allow you to get away with any misbehaviors. As your husband and your papa, it is my responsibility not only to care for you, but to correct you when you've done wrong." He tipped her chin up, forcing her to stare into his dark, stern gaze. "Do you understand, little Cammie?"

"I-I understand, sir." She swallowed past the sudden dryness in her mouth. Her heart raced faster and faster. Despite her current predicament, a quick, heated spasm afflicted the area between her legs.

She squirmed in place under the scolding look her papa had leveled upon her. Would he spank her? Or would he make her stand in a corner to contemplate her misdeeds? If he hadn't been holding her gaze, she would have spared a glance around the room for something that resembled a naughty chair. She knew only one thing for certain.

She'd been a wayward little girl, and her new papa, the handsome but no nonsense Lord Cavendish, was about to punish her for the very first time.

CHAPTER 4

Alexander stared down at his little Cammie, contemplating how to best chastise her for her naughtiness. He couldn't allow her off with a warning. Not even this first time. No, a warning simply would not do. He had to impress upon her the importance of obedience from the start of their marriage.

Even if they weren't technically married yet.

He stepped back from his soon-to-be bride and glanced at the clock. They still had a few hours until the vicar's arrival. He ought to punish her now and get it over with.

He opened his mouth to order Cammie into the corner, but suddenly the past came rushing back. The last time he'd ordered a young lady to stand in a corner as punishment, Lady Honoria to be exact, she had rejected him and run off. What if Cammie changed her mind once he set about chastising her and decided to return back to Talcott House with Miss Wickersham? He wasn't sure he could bear it. His heart felt heavy at the thought of losing the pretty little girl with the large brown eyes that seemed to call to his soul.

"Sir?" Cammie asked, her expression uncertain.

"Yes, my dear?"

"If you, um, have a naughty chair, I will go sit on it. I…I am truly sorry to have disappointed you."

Naughty chair? His interest piqued, he narrowed his eyes at her. At the same time, his heart rejoiced. Sitting on a naughty chair was similar to standing in a corner, and she seemed willing to take her punishment. "Is that how Miss Wickersham deals with you when you've been naughty? Sends you to sit in a naughty chair?"

"Well, sir, sometimes." She appeared to be hesitating, and twisted her fingers together, fidgeting in place as she glanced from side to side. A sheen of moisture glistened in her eyes. "It's just, *please oh please* don't give me a spanking, sir. Not today. Tomorrow, perhaps, if you must. But please not today."

She reached around herself and cupped her bottom cheeks in the most adorable manner.

"Cammie, why don't you want a spanking today? We're to be married in a mere few hours. Is it that you don't wish for me to lay a hand on you until we are wed? Or is there another reason? I want the truth. We must be honest with one another, or our marriage will surely fail."

Still cupping her bottom cheeks, she peered up at him with a look of increasing trepidation. "Oh, please, sir. Please don't make me tell you why."

"Cammie," he said kindly, though with a certain amount of steel in his voice, "I am starting to think something is terribly wrong, and I am worried for you. You will tell me what is the matter this instant. Start talking. Now."

She finally released her bottom and crossed her arms over her chest, hugging herself. "I-I am usually a very, very well-behaved little girl. I swear it. But yesterday I got in trouble with the nurse and got a spanking. My bottom is still quite sore, and I suspect it's probably still a bit pinkened, sir, and I'm mortified by the prospect of you seeing it. I am ashamed to come to you like this, sir, with an already punished bottom. I hope you won't think I'm always into trouble and decide to send me back to Talcott House. Oh please, please just make me sit on a naughty chair. Or stand in a corner. Spank me tomorrow, if you must, but please don't lift my skirts and add to my soreness just yet." She sniffled and lowered her head. A lone tear carved a path down her cheek, and Alexander found himself moving forward to brush that tear away.

He gathered her close to his chest, and she soon loosened her arms, letting them fall to her sides and allowing him to hold her closer and tighter. God, he loved the feel of her in his arms. He rested his chin atop her head. She fit against him perfectly. As if they were meant to be. His heart broke knowing she still harbored doubts that he would keep her. Twice now she had voiced her concerns that he might send her back to Talcott House. Didn't she know he'd been waiting for her for what felt like forever? Didn't she know how eagerly he'd anticipated this day—the day they would become husband and wife, papa and little girl?

"Cammie," he said in the most soothing tone he could muster. "You're mine now. My little girl. I will never, ever get rid of you. Would that I could banish the fear from your mind." He kissed the top of her head, letting his lips linger and inhaling the floral scent of her hair. "Now, about the spanking you received yesterday. I want to know what you did to earn yourself a punishment, little girl." He led her to the sofa and bid her to sit down. Once she sank onto the cushion, he clasped her hands in his and stared at her intently, willing her to confess her misdeeds.

"Well, sir, first I back talked one of the caregivers, when she told me to go see the nurse. I was having fun talking to my friends and I didn't want to visit the nurse, plus I wasn't feeling ill, so I didn't think she could have any good reason to call for me."

"I see. And what did the nurse call you for?"

Cammie's face reddened, and she glanced away from him, as if embarrassed to admit the reason the nurse had called for her. Just when he was about to prompt her again, she took a deep breath and met his eyes. "She wanted to give me a medical exam, to make sure I would be healthy and to ensure I would be a good wife to you, sir. I, um, didn't wish to take all my clothes off and get on the exam table, and she had to undress me herself. As you might imagine, she was not pleased, and she smacked my bare bottom hard, again and again. Even once I got up onto the table, she still continued the spanking." As she spoke, Cammie squirmed in her seat.

The description of his little girl getting a spanking from her nurse had an immediate and dire effect on Alexander. In fact, he didn't think he would be able to stand up for quite some time. His cock had grown hard as a rock while he listened to Cammie's confession, and his mind had painted a pretty picture of her standing naked in the nurse's office, while the nurse swatted her bare behind and then continued to spank her once she'd gotten up onto the table. A thought struck him, and he had to know the answer, no matter how inappropriate the question might be, given that they weren't officially yet husband and wife.

"Did the nurse look upon your privates, Cammie?"

Her eyes went wide. "Yes, sir. First she shaved me, um, *down there,* and then she gave me a most thorough examination. As I said, she wanted to ensure that you would find me pleasing. She was especially satisfied when my cunny became wet when she touched it, sir."

Alexander started coughing and sat back, covering his mouth. God's teeth. Did Cammie have any idea the effect she was having on him? He was entertaining some most ungentlemanly thoughts toward her in this moment. He wanted to turn her over his knee, bare her bottom, and inspect the nurse's handiwork. Then he wanted to stroke the delicate pink folds of his naughty little girl's quim, until a release shuddered through her.

He took several deep breaths and thought of England, trying to contain his lust. He cleared his throat and stared into her expressive, innocent dark gaze. Clearly, she had no idea his cock had swelled rigid within the confines of his trousers.

"Cammie, I already find you pleasing. Tell me, did the nurse touch your bum hole?"

"No, sir, but Miss Wickersham did when she came to assist the nurse. She was the one to take my temperature."

The mental image of prim and proper Miss Wickersham taking part in such an intimate examination and inserting a thermometer into Cammie's rosebud did nothing to abate his building desires. Alexander shifted in his seat and inhaled another calming breath. But he felt anything but settled as he continued to hold his sweet little girl's gaze. Had her pucker winked at Miss Wickersham while the older woman pushed the thermometer inside? Had Cammie trembled with yet unknown desires on the table while the nurse touched her cunny and made it grow wet?

He stood up suddenly, facing away from Cammie, lest she notice the bulge tenting the front of his trousers. Thankfully, standing and staring out the window seemed to help, and after a while, he had gathered himself enough to turn around and face his little bride yet again.

"Thank you for telling me the reason you received a spanking yesterday, Cammie. Now, back to what we were discussing a few moments ago. You disobeyed Miss Wickersham's instructions to remain in this room, and for that, young lady, you will be punished." He nodded at the vacant corner to his right. "You will stand in that corner, with your nose touching the wall, until I decide you've had a long enough time to contemplate your misdeeds."

Her breath caught in a gasp and she stared at him, unmoving, as her eyes grew wider and wider. Had he spoken too sternly and scared her? For a moment, doubts swept through his mind, and his heart pounded with worry. But no, he couldn't coddle her in this moment. She had earned her first punishment as his bride, never mind that they hadn't spoken their vows yet, and he had a duty to guide her to the best of his ability, as a good papa ought to guide his little girl.

"If I must put you in the corner myself, I will smack your bottom the entire way there, young lady."

His threat propelled her into action. She jumped off the couch and strode to the corner, putting her nose against the wall as instructed.

"Good girl. Now, once we are wed, most of your corner time will be spent naked, or at the very least with skirts raised and your bottom bared, while waiting for a spanking. However, since we haven't spoken our vows yet, I will allow you to maintain your modesty." He walked closer to her and grabbed ahold of her hips. "Jut your behind out a bit. Think about how the next time you misbehave, you'll find yourself standing naked in a corner, waiting for your papa to come tend to your naughty bare bottom."

A tremor ran through her, but she obeyed, angling her bottom out.

Then he cupped her behind, a bold move that surprised even him.

"Tonight, you will share my bed. I will see you unclothed, little Cammie, and I can assure you, I will be inspecting your bare bottom for any lingering redness from the spanking the nurse gave you. I realize that might embarrass you, but I'm to be your husband and your papa, and there will be no secrets between us."

"Yes, sir. I understand."

"Papa. Call me Papa, Cammie."

"Yes, Papa."

Papa. How he had longed for a little miss to call him Papa and Cammie was even more perfect than he had ever dared to hope. Miss Wickersham had a reputation for sweet young ladies who had been reared in her care to yearn for a papa, but he had never really believed it was possible for her to make a match which suited him immediately.

"How old are you, Cammie?" he asked suddenly. Miss Wickersham had assured him the girl was of age, but Cammie was rather petite.

"Poor nutrition, not to mention frequent bouts of starvation, often inhibits proper growth in children," Miss Wickersham had said with an imperious sniff when he had commented on Cammie's size. He had felt properly chastened, but still wished to affirm the girl's age. He was not one to tamper with children.

"I am nineteen, Papa," she replied, her nose still pressed to the diverging walls of the corner.

"Nineteen," he repeated, stepping back to admire the position she'd taken up with only minimal prompting and no arguments whatsoever. It pleased him that she was amenable to receiving discipline, even physical correction. He couldn't wait to strip off her dress later and inspect every inch of her luscious little body, including her bare behind. Perhaps he would give her a few playful swats in the bedroom, to help her become accustomed to his expectations in a bride and help her feel more comfortable when the time finally came that he must give her a well-earned spanking.

"I realize I am young, Papa, but I can assure you that I'm very grown up. I am ready to become a wife. Nurse Lister also explained to me how babies are made. I know you must stick your, um, penis inside my cunny. I promise to hold my legs wide apart and be a good girl and hold very still while you do that."

Christ. The things she said. Her innocent, sweet promise to hold still while he claimed her as his bride made his cock thicken again. He returned his hand to her bottom and gave it a squeeze. "I can promise you, little Cammie, that whatever technical explanation the nurse gave you was woefully lacking. I will teach you all you need to know in the bedroom, but know that I will require your complete obedience. If I ask you to do something and you refuse, you will be punished. Now, no more talking until I give you permission to speak. You will remain in this position for as long as it pleases me, thinking about how naughty it was of you to disobey Miss Wickersham's instructions to remain in this room. I also want you to think about how the next time you misbehave, you will go over your papa's knee for a hard, shameful spanking on your bare little bottom."

A small gasp left her, but she wisely didn't utter a word.

~

LORD CAVENDISH—NO, *Papa*—had put her in the corner. Not only that, but he'd promised to spank her bare bottom the next time she was naughty. Oh, and tonight he would see her naked and stick his penis—whatever that was—inside her. Her mind swirled and she felt faint as she tried to hold the increasingly uncomfortable position in the corner.

Her stomach flipped. What if Miss Wickersham returned with the vicar early, only to find her charge already in trouble with her new papa? She hoped Papa called her out of the corner soon. Worry began to gnaw at her as the minutes ticked by. It shamed her that her bottom was jutted out in a most unladylike manner, and when her papa had squeezed her behind, he'd reinvigorated the sting leftover from the spanking Nurse Lister had given her yesterday.

She gave an impatient sigh, frustrated that she couldn't seem to control herself. To make matters worse, she was having a difficult time holding still with her nose pressed to the wall and her cunny feeling achier by the second. What she wouldn't give to straighten and press her legs close together to relieve the building ache. Perhaps when Lord Cavendish and Miss Wickersham had left this room earlier, her time would have been better spent stroking that deliciously sensitive nubbin hidden within the folds of her cunny, rather than leaving the room and getting herself locked out of the house. They'd left her alone long enough for her to have had time to pleasure herself, but now, here she was in the corner, despite trying to do the right thing and avoid punishment in the first place.

The indignity and unfairness of her situation prompted her to sigh again, louder this time, and even go so far as to stomp her foot, as if she were a naughty child in the midst of a temper tantrum.

"Cammie, that's enough." Her papa didn't sound the least bit pleased by her theatrics. "I thought a corner time punishment would be welcome, as far as chastisements go, especially considering that your bottom is still sore from your recent spanking at Talcott House, but it appears you don't appreciate the leniency I tried to show you. I assure you, the rest of your time spent in this room will be most uncomfortable. Now, come here."

Oh no. What had she done? Her tummy flipped as she turned around to face her stony-faced papa. Fear wound through her, and while she still felt safe being alone with Lord Cavendish, she didn't think she would like what was about to happen.

He removed his jacket, laying it on the couch, and began to roll his sleeves up in a methodical manner, keeping his stern gaze fixed on her.

"As I have said, I will not tolerate a disobedient little girl. I realize your bottom might still be pinkened from yesterday's spanking, but that's not going to stop me adding to it and giving you the correction you so richly deserve. Given your huffing and stomping, it's my opinion that Nurse Lister did not spank you nearly hard and long enough. I intend to remedy that right now, Cammie. You have left me no choice," he said as he finished rolling up his sleeves.

As his words sank in and her anxieties grew, she found herself staring at his thick manly forearms, along with his large hands. Oh dear. His hands were a lot larger than Nurse Lister's or Miss Wickersham's. She gulped, and a second later, her hands flew behind her as she attempted to shield her bottom.

"Oh, Papa! I'm so sorry. But you made me stand in the corner for a long, long time. And it's not fair," she said, resisting the urge to stomp again. "I mean, if I hadn't gone outside to smell the flowers, I would have likely gotten into trouble in this room.

He arched an eyebrow at her. "What kind of trouble, young lady?"

Her eyes widened and she could have kicked herself for not being quiet.

"Cammie..."

She crossed her arms and lifted her chin, trying to look like a big girl. But his jaw soon tightened and she knew if she didn't confess what kind of trouble she'd been referring to, he would likely attempt to spank the truth out of her. Oh, but it was so shameful, to admit out loud that she'd been tempted to touch her own cunny. What would her papa think?

He took a step toward her and she backed up, putting her

hands up in a show of surrender. Very well. She would confess the naughty thoughts that had flitted through her mind. The temptation that she had tried very hard to resist this afternoon, though she hadn't been able to resist it last night, when she stroked herself to bliss in secret under her bed covers.

"Fine," she said, in a much more subdued tone. "If you must know, I became achy between my thighs, as I had yesterday during my examination. I thought about touching myself, to make the aching feel better, but I soon decided that wouldn't be proper and since I was still missing my friend and feeling a little uneasy about all the change that's happening, I went outside rather than stay in here and risk doing something I suppose you wouldn't approve of me doing. It's against the rules to touch our kitties in Talcott House, as Miss Wickersham says we must save our special gifts for our papas." She spoke in a rush, hoping Papa would show her some additional leniency for her honesty. She stole a peek at him, but his face remained unreadable.

Her heart hammered in her chest as she awaited his response. Did he understand and see her side of things? Or was he even more displeased with her now that she'd confessed to having wayward thoughts?

"Thank you for telling me the full truth, Cammie," he finally said, his features softening. "Miss Wickersham is right in that regard. A young lady's cunny is a special gift that belongs to her papa, and you are never to touch yourself there without permission." He approached her and cupped her face, and she practically melted at the warmth of his large hands holding her in such a tender fashion, as if she were the most special girl in the world to him. Her heart fluttered and the heated throbbing between her thighs restarted.

She yearned for his touch with every fiber of her being, and suddenly there wasn't enough air in the room. She took a couple of deep, shuddering breaths in an effort to calm herself and not drift back into her salacious musings while he was speaking to her. Whatever Papa was about to say must be important, because the lines on his forehead creased and his mouth tightened slightly before his lips parted on a quick inhale.

"Little girl, if you ever touch your kitty without permission, Papa will force your legs apart and smack the delicate folds of your privates. A long, hard spanking on your kitty is what will happen if I ever catch you in the midst of such naughtiness. Do you understand?"

"Of course, Papa. I-I understand. I won't dare touch my quim." Oh heavens. A spanking on her privates. She couldn't even imagine the shame of enduring such an intimate punishment, even if it were delivered by her papa, and she trembled at the idea of having to spread her legs and await each stinging smack to her tender folds.

His lips tightened again. "You're my little girl, and I think quim and cunny are much too grownup of words for you to use. Unless I tell you otherwise, you're to call your privates your kitty. Now, I don't feel it's appropriate to have you squirming over my lap when we are yet unmarried, so I want you to be a good girl and bend over the arm of the couch instead. I haven't forgotten your misbehavior in the corner. I know a certain little girl who's going to have a bright red bottom while she's saying her wedding vows."

CHAPTER 5

Her obedience pleased him. More than he had imagined it would. Little Cammie rested over the arm of the couch, emitting the occasional nervous whimper, but otherwise remaining quiet and still.

He placed a hand on her bottom. "Young lady, I am going to make this quick but hard. You will learn to follow directions, and you will learn to control your temper and show more patience, or else you will find yourself in this position more often than you would like. Had you remained in the corner, as quiet and still as you are being right now, you would likely be snuggling in my lap at this very moment, rather than finding yourself bent over a couch awaiting your papa to redden your bare little bottom."

She gasped, but before she had a chance to move, he flipped up her skirts and her chemise, then parted the slit of her drawers, revealing her nakedness. His blood heated. God, she was a lovely creature. He spread her drawers wider apart, letting his fingertips trail across her pale flesh. Inspecting her, he saw just a hint of pinkness on her lower left cheek, the only evidence that she'd endured a recent punishment.

Of course, her entire bottom would be reddened by the time he was finished with her.

He still couldn't believe she'd had the audacity to huff and stomp her foot. Had she been testing him to see if he really would spank her? Or was she simply unable to control herself when she became frustrated? Well, he supposed it didn't matter, because either way, she was about to be on the receiving end of a good hard bottom smacking.

Standing beside her, he placed a firm hand on her lower back and raised his other hand, preparing his aim. He brought his flattened palm down upon her right buttock first, then quickly slapped her left one. She wiggled and gasped, but he continued on, spanking her with hardly a pause between slaps. Her curvy little cheeks soon pinkened, and then reddened, under his chastising swats.

"Ouch ouch ouch!" she cried. "Oh, Papa, I'm so sorry! Please no more spanking!"

"Your punishment will continue until I'm satisfied that you have indeed learned your lesson, little girl. Papa is in charge here, not you, young lady. You would do well to remember that."

She whimpered and her shoulders heaved. A moment later, he heard the sound of sniffles followed by a heartfelt sob that wrenched at his soul. He gave her three more slaps, then stopped and rubbed her punished cheeks, deciding she had indeed had enough.

"Shh, sweet girl. It's over now. You took your punishment well."

He fixed her drawers back into place and gave her behind an affectionate pat. Then he returned her skirts and chemise to rights and lifted her off the sofa, only to draw her directly into his lap after he sank down on the cushions. He wrapped his arms around her and was pleased when she returned his hug and nestled her head against his chest.

"Do you know why you got a spanking, Cammie?"

"Y-yes, Papa. I was a bad girl."

Alexander swiftly shifted position so he could look into her eyes when next he spoke. "You were not a bad girl, Cammie. You will never be a bad girl. Bad girl is a phrase we do not use in this household. Do you understand that?"

Her soft brows furrowed over her eyes. "B-but you punished me."

"You were not bad. You were naughty, a very naughty girl indeed." He took note of the way her breath hitched when he called her naughty. He stifled the happy smile that wanted to burst upon his lips for it would not do to have her know how much it pleased him. "You are a good girl. You are Papa's good little girl. And sometimes good girls do naughty things or even bad things, but that does not make them bad."

She thought for a minute and pursed her lips in concentration before resting her head against his shoulder and smiling up at him. "I think I understand, Papa. Thank you for explaining it to me so well." She sighed. "I think I am going to like having you as my papa."

He pulled her close and held her for a moment, planting a kiss upon her forehead.

"All is forgiven, my little poppet."

"Thank you, Papa. I will try to be good from now on. I would not like to disappoint you again," she said, gazing up at him solemnly. Her trust melted his heart.

"That is the point of punishment, my dear. Once the penalty has been imposed, the deed is forgotten, and we may continue as husband and wife in a happy manner, without the cloud of disappointment or worry hanging over us. Does that make sense to you?"

He watched as she pondered his words until she met his gaze and said, with a small smile, "Yes, Papa, I understand. I think your idea is a good one. Thank you for thinking of it."

He dropped another kiss atop her head. Though he longed to wrap her snuggly in his arms and probe her pink lips with his own, he did not wish to alarm the poor girl. She had already traveled a great distance from her home in the country to the bustling streets of London, not to mention the naughty desires he had for her, his one wish was to make her feel safe and content in his home.

"Now," he said, standing and taking her hand in his, "let us not talk of such unpleasantness. Would you care for a tour of Ashton Manor, your new home?"

"Oh, yes." Her eyes glistened with excitement. "I would like that very much, Papa."

He assisted her in climbing the large staircase that led to the second floor of Ashton Manor then down a long corridor to her room. He held his breath in excited anticipation, hoping against hope that she would be pleased with the arrangements he had made for her. Opening the door, he watched her face as the room was revealed to her one small part at a time.

Her eyes popped and her mouth fell open as she stepped across the threshold and then into the center of the room. Speechless, she turned in a slow circle taking in what he hoped was the perfect room for his little girl.

"D-do you like it?" he asked, nervous as a schoolboy as he awaited her response.

She circled again, this time more slowly and she made a wider circumnavigation of the room, reaching out to touch a lace covered table here or a porcelain doll there. Hesitantly, she moved to the corner where a large dollhouse stood, an exact replica of Ashton Manor. She turned to look at him and moved her lips, but no sound came out.

"Cammie? Are you well?" Crossing the room, he clasped her hands in his, staring down into her beautiful face.

"Y-yes, Papa," she finally said on a whisper. "I-I have never seen anything so grand in my entire life. Is this really meant to be my room?"

His heart soared with happiness to see her astonishment at his creation. "Yes," he said. "Yours and yours alone."

"At Talcott House, I shared a room, with Hyacinth, Daisy and Rosie."

"Did all of the other girls at Talcott House have flower names? Cammie is not a flower," he said.

"Yes," she said. "Miss Wickersham gave everyone a new name when they came to live with her at Talcott House. She said we were her little blossoms. And," she added with a giggle, clearly pleased at having a surprise for him, "my name is Camellia, but everyone calls me Cammie, but that's a flower too."

"So it is." He smiled down at her, his pleasure in her company increasing every moment.

Alexander was curious about what had brought his little Cammie to live at Talcott House, but he was not so sure he wished to ask at this time. Miss Wickersham had told him a small amount, that her brother had been about to sell Cammie off as a servant girl to a disreputable household. He shivered at the idea of anyone else laying claim to his little treasure, and fierce anger coursed through his veins at the thought of her working her fingers to the bone day after day. Much as Miss Wickersham annoyed him with her brusque manner and humorless ways, he had to acknowledge the importance of her mission. A mission which had brought sweet Cammie to him.

"I am glad the room pleases you, Cammie," he said, but then noticed that she seemed confused about something. "Is everything to your liking, Cammie girl? You look upset."

She worried her bottom lip between her teeth and his cock stirred in his trousers imagining those same lips wrapped around his hard member, but he forced those thoughts away. His first priority was to assure his Cammie's comfort and happiness.

"I-I thought that m-married people...well, Rosie said that...and bossy Garland too...they all said that well, that little girls and papas shared a b-bed, and I thought you said something similar downstairs, but perhaps I misheard you." Having said what was on her mind, Cammie turned from him and buried her face in her small hands, an adorable flush visible on the back of her neck.

Gently, he placed his hands on her shoulders and turned her to face him, lowering her hands so they could look at each other.

"That is true," he said, "and I am looking forward to sharing my bed with you tonight, after we are married." He felt her quiver in his hands and pulled her to him, stroking his palm down the length of her back and forcing himself to stop before continuing down to cup the curves of her bottom. "In my bed, you will be my wife, a grown up lady. Lady Cavendish. But here, in your room, is where you will be my little girl, my sweet Cammie. Does that make sense to you?"

He held his breath while she considered his words. "I-I think it does," she said. "I am to be your little girl, but also your wife." She blushed again, but this time she did not turn away, so Alexander felt he was making some progress.

"Exactly," he said. "This room is yours where you can play and keep your little girl things." He led her to a door along the wall. "In here," he opened the door to display a dressing area filled with dresses of all description, some more fitting for little Cammie and others for Lady Cavendish. She gasped and gaped at the collection of fabrics and laces.

"Are these all for me?" she asked, astonished.

CAMMIE WONDERED if she might faint dead away. An entire room filled with clothes and shoes, hats, capes, and other things she could not even identify. Miss Wickersham had certainly done her best to outfit her little charges, and Cammie had been grateful for two or three dresses which were laundered on a regular basis. Sometimes, late at night, she had memories of her time before arriving at Miss Wickersham's and how she wore an old dress that was torn and dirty and how people looked right through her as though she did not exist, or if they did look at her, they turned their heads and glanced the other way. Only Miss Wickersham had seen fit to offer her clean clothes and treat her with dignity.

And now, Miss Wickersham had found her a papa who wanted to treat her like a princess. His princess. There really was no other way to describe it. She wondered if royalty had as many clothes as she saw hanging about.

A small fabric covered stool stood in the center of the room. "What is that for, Papa?" she asked.

With an over-exaggerated bow, he extended his hand to her. "Step this way and find out, my lady."

She giggled and placed her hand in his. Oh, how she loved the feel of his strong fingers around hers. He led her over and helped her to step up on the stool. "This," he said, "is where you will stand while I assist you in dressing for the day."

Cammie gasped. "Y-you will assist me in dressing? Is that not a servant's job?"

"That is true, my little treasure, but it is my pleasure and my duty to take care of you, to take care of all your needs and that includes helping you dress."

"W-will I not have a maid for such things?"

"On those rare occasions when I cannot attend to my responsibilities as your papa, one of the house maids will take over those duties, but only on a temporary basis. You, my dear sweet Cammie, are mine and I shall shower you with all of the love and attention you have ever wanted. And that I have always wanted to shower upon my own little bride."

Cammie's head spun with the notion of her papa dressing and undressing her every day, assisting her with her clothing. A soft giggle escaped her lips.

"What is so funny, Cammie?" Papa asked, a smile on his face.

"Will you also style my hair, Papa?"

"Oh, you are a sassy one, are you not?" Papa gave her hair a playful tug. "I might surprise you with my skills."

Cammie giggled again and peeked up at her papa from beneath her lashes. He was certainly a handsome man and that funny tingly feeling had returned. Or perhaps it had never left. Standing on the stool, she wiggled a little bit from side to side.

"Would you like to try on one of your new dresses, Cammie?" Papa asked with a gleam in his eye. "I would very much like to see you in some of the items I selected for you. I have a particular ensemble in mind for our wedding ceremony."

A joyful smile covered her face. "Oh, yes, Papa. I would like that very much. It was a long trip here today and fresh clothing would make me very happy. Besides," she glanced up at him with a saucy look, "I wish for you to be happy as well."

"It would make me very happy." He reached behind her to work the closures on her traveling dress and when he did, it brought him ever so close to her.

The ninnies on her breasts got hard and rubbed against the fabric of her chemise and the tingly feeling got stronger. Papa had opened all the closures on her dress and slowly lowered it. Cammie's breath caught in her throat as he worked the gown down her body, first revealing her shoulders and then tugging the sleeves until her arms were bare, leaving the bodice of her dress resting along her hips. Cammie snuck a peek downward, her breasts felt heavy and the tips ached. Why was her body acting so strangely? She swallowed hard and tried to compose herself.

Looking up into her papa's face, she saw he was staring at her breasts. She worried her lip before whispering, "I am sorry, Papa."

"Why are you sorry, sweet Cammie?"

"M-my ni-ninnies are all hard. It feels funny. I wonder if there is something w-wrong with me." She turned her face away, unable to bear his scrutiny and horrified by what his response might be.

His fingertips brushed gently along the fabric over her breasts, sending a jolt of heat directly to her lady parts, and she squirmed in place atop the upholstered stool. "Oh, Papa, what is that? What is wrong with me?"

"There is not one thing wrong with you, my dear Cammie." Papa's voice sounded funny, sort of husky and emotional and Cammie saw him lick his lips while he gazed upon her fabric covered breasts.

"B-but, Papa," she insisted, "I feel so strange, sort of hot and then tingly and I am sure I must have the flu or something. Oh, Papa, I am so sorry. Please do not send me back with Miss Wickersham. I am certain I will feel better in just a few days and then we can enjoy ourselves."

Papa chuckled and cupped her face with his strong palms, forcing her eyes to meet his. "Do you feel tingly down between your legs as well?"

"Y-yes, Papa," she said, shamefaced. "I feel like I am leaking down there too."

"Hmm. You had better let me take a look." He released her

face and proceeded to lift her chemise from her ankles, to her knees and higher.

By the time he raised it and parted her drawers to expose her moisture laden lady parts, Cammie was in a frenzy of embarrassment and achy longing. She alternated between biting her lip and crying out in undecipherable moans.

When she stood before him and he had exposed her feminine parts, Cammie covered herself with her hands, but Papa gently moved them away. "You will not hide from me, little Cammie. All of your body is mine, and I shall gaze upon it whenever I so choose. Do you understand?"

"Y-yes, Papa."

"Your body is beautiful, and it makes me happy to be able to look at it and touch it. There is nothing for you to be ashamed of."

"Y-yes, Papa."

She watched as her papa took her chemise and carefully lowered it toward her knees. She wished he would touch her some more, but she dared not say so, it would be too shameful to voice such things aloud. Besides, she enjoyed the opportunity to study him as he carefully moved the chemise down her stocking covered legs.

He reached up beneath her chemise and untied the ribbons holding her stockings in place and they fell around her ankles.

CHAPTER 6

Alexander, Lord Cavendish, had completely lost his mind. That was what he told himself and he tended to believe it. He had turned his back on her, in part to fold her clothes in a tidy fashion, but mostly to keep himself from taking her tiny little body and plastering it against his hard cock until he pounded into the sweet juices of her virgin cunny over and over again, breaking her in and making her his forever.

But he could not behave that way. Not yet, anyway. The poor thing had only been at his house for less than two hours and they had been alone for less than sixty minutes. Despite that, he felt an uncontrollable urge, as though he had known her his entire life, but that still did not allow him to forego all semblance of gentlemanlike behavior and act like a madman gone a rutting.

Particularly not with his sweet, delicate, little flower, Camellia. His Cammie. Blocking her view of him with his back, he buried his face in her clothing, inhaling the sweet scent of her, a combination of innocence and untried passion. He felt himself getting hard again and wondered how he would survive the few hours until Miss Wickersham returned with the vicar.

Giving himself a mental shake and an internal monologue of rebuke, Alexander completed the task of stowing her clothes by carefully rolling up her stockings, the delicate wisp of fabric which had encased her adorable feet, noting that she'd torn a hole in them, likely during her adventures outside. He decided not to mention it, as he'd already punished her for that episode of naughtiness. All had been forgiven, and to his delight, she didn't seemed outraged in the least that he'd disciplined her.

Truly, she was meant to be his adorable little bride.

He sat on a nearby chair facing her, then patted his lap and she obediently stepped down from the stool, dressed in nothing but the thin chemise, and walked over to stand in front of him. He opened his legs and pulled her closer, taking her two hands in his. They were face to face and he could see she was upset, which surprised him, as he'd thought the matter of her shyness and modesty had been resolved and that he had given her sufficient assurances so she felt comfortable with him dressing and undressing her. Yet a small tear rolled down her cheek. He wiped it away with the pad of his thumb. He felt her inhale sharply and her face pinkened. Perhaps she was simply nervous, or embarrassed at being practically naked in front of him for the first time. She shuddered and gave a little gasp.

"Does my touch excite you, my sweet Cammie?"

"I-I do not know," she said, unable to meet his gaze. "When you touch me, I feel warm, all over. And sometimes I have a funny tingly feeling in my tummy. And my ninnies. They tingle and ache even worse than earlier. Oh, Papa. It feels as though my body has a mind of its own and I cannot manage it. Are you certain I am not ill?"

"No, little poppet." He cupped her face in his hands, "You

are not ill. This is called arousal. It is what you ought to feel for your papa."

"B-but, I felt it before I met you, too. It started yesterday and maybe the day before, when Miss Wickersham told me I had a papa, but I did not know you at the time."

"Well, it sounds as though you have a desire for a papa to take care of you and to help you make that tingle go away, at least temporarily."

She squirmed from side to side. "The tingle is getting worse, Papa."

~

CAMMIE LEANED her head on Papa's shoulder and sighed contentedly after he pulled her onto his lap. His arms wrapped around her like a warm blanket of safety and peace. He smelled good too. Like soap and fresh air. She slipped her arms around his waist and snuggled as close as she could.

Papa seemed to like that because he tightened his grip too, though he also moved around a little bit on the chair. There was something hard in his trousers. It poked against Cammie's bottom and it made her want to squirm.

Papa still had not told her how he was going to make the tingling in her kitty go away, and the tingling had morphed into an urgent longing spreading all through her body. It seemed that sitting on Papa's lap, especially with the firm rod that she could feel through his trousers, made everything heat up and throb.

It made Cammie feel unsettled, verging on out of control, characteristics which Miss Wickersham and others at Talcott House had put forth significant effort to abolish in all the residents, including Cammie. A proper lady was placid and refined in all her actions and thoughts. She must always give the outward appearance of serenity.

That particular lesson had been one of the most difficult for Cammie, but she worked hard and had believed she had mastered the technique of a tranquil ladylike demeanor. But ever since her visit to Nurse Lister's office, there had been an awakening of new urges and yearnings, aches in her ninnies and kitty that seemed to have taken over her ability to think clearly or behave as she had been taught. The urges had caused her to break one of the most important rules of Talcott House. Miss Wickersham had very strictly monitored her girls and she did not permit any touching of their private parts other than for the most perfunctory needs. Dire warnings had been given of the results of not obeying that rule that were enough to keep Cammie from exploring, though she suspected others had tested the limits of the rule based upon some of the wriggling and moaning she sometimes detected from the adjoining beds after lights out.

Until the night before, Cammie had been too fearful of the repercussions. She had carefully scrutinized her friends and none had exhibited the hairy palms or blindness which had been predicted. Still, she hadn't dared to take the risk until recently. Miss Wickersham had promised to find the best papas for her girls who obeyed the rules and Cammie was certain her papa was the best of the best. It made her proud that she had behaved—most of the time, at least. Now she felt ashamed for having touched herself in secret underneath her covers on her last night at Talcott House. But more than that, she feared for the fact that she no longer had dominion over her body and its reactions.

Miss Wickersham had worked hard to train her to behave as a proper lady ought. Much of society believed that breeding and lineage determined whether someone could move in the upper circles of society, but Miss Wickersham believed anyone could become a member of high society with the proper training.

Cammie had only been away from Talcott House for a few hours, and already her ladylike demeanor was slipping away. How could she ever be a proper wife for Lord Cavendish? Could she truly live up to the title of Lady Cavendish?

Papa had said he knew what to do about the tingling and the jittery sensations she had, though she dared not ask him to relieve them lest he know how little self-control she had. But it was getting stronger and stronger. Would he touch her directly on her kitty again? Or was there another way to make the aching stop? It seemed, despite Papa's explanations and her rather enlightening trip to Nurse Lister's office yesterday, there were still many mysteries of the body she didn't understand.

Cammie clenched her thighs together creating pressure on her kitty and that seemed to alleviate the tingling some, but not all of it. She noticed that when she wiggled over the hard thing Papa had in his trousers, the tingling seemed to get better and some of the ache inside of her calmed.

She continued rubbing back and forth on the solid rod beneath her, and she had almost forgotten about Papa, the feelings flowing through her veins were so intense. Suddenly Papa grabbed her by the upper arms and set her on her feet in front of him.

"Camellia!" he said, his face flushed and eyes wild. "Have mercy on me."

The tingling was forgotten and she gaped up at Papa. "W-what have I done? Oh, Papa, please do not be angry with me."

She stepped back from him and took in his entire countenance. His hands were clenched at his sides, and he appeared to be biting his lip as though forcing himself to retain his composure. Oh dear. Surely she had done something to infuriate him and he was on the verge of exploding in anger. Would he give her another spanking? Or would he decide she was too much trouble, after all, and send her back to Talcott House?

Too frightened to think or know what to do, Cammie ran from the room, through the large dressing area, past all of the pretty dresses, capes and shoes, and through the door at the other side. The room she entered was completely unexpected.

Inside the room was a huge bed which seemed to take up the entire room, though, of course, it did not. This room was large and masculine, filled with leather covered furniture and clothing which was undoubtedly manly. Cammie stopped short when she crossed the threshold and gaped at the sight before her.

Papa was soon at her side, his hand resting gently on the lower part of her back, just above her punished bottom. "This," he said in a raspy whisper, "is my bedchamber. Here we will spend our wedding night, and all of our nights. This is where you will become my bride, my wife. As a woman. Not a little girl. Do you understand, Cammie?"

A bout of anxiety rattled her body and Papa's hand at the small of her back seemed to burn through her chemise and heated her flesh all over the skin below her waist. "I-I believe I understand, Papa." She bit her lip and then turned to him. "Nurse Lister explained to me about the-the penis and my kitty, but I am beginning to believe there is more to it than that. I-I trust you to help me with the parts I do not understand. You will help me, will you not, Papa?"

The smile that spread across his face and lit up his eyes filled Cammie with joy. "Yes, Cammie, I will absolutely help you to understand. I want nothing more than for you to be happy, particularly in my bed."

~

ALEXANDER COULD BARELY TEAR his gaze away from his little bride and forced himself not to toss her upon the bed and defile her. Christ. And she was wearing nothing but a thin chemise. If he managed to leave her unclaimed before they actually spoke their vows, it would be a miracle. Still, he resolved to be a gentleman, even if his balls had tightened something fierce and his cock kept lurching in protest.

"Miss Wickersham and the vicar will be here soon, Cammie," he said. "We must get you dressed in a proper gown for your wedding."

"Oh yes, Papa." She clasped her hands and turned to face him. "Thank you ever so much for all of the beautiful clothes. You shall spoil me."

"That is my intention," he said, leading her back into the dressing area between their rooms and lifting her to stand upon the stool. He whisked away the chemise and allowed himself the briefest of glances at her nudity. His breath caught in his throat and heat fired in his loins, but he forced himself to gather up clothing and cover her as quickly as possible. Once he had covered her with a chemise, stockings and other proper undergarments, he felt he could look upon her without losing control of his lust.

He knew precisely the dress he wished for his little bride to wear and found it quickly. White with handmade lace around the collar, hem and cuffs, the dress had cost him a small fortune, and he had quickly had it altered in the two days since Miss Wickersham's visit in order for it to fit his precious Cammie. Sliding the garment over her head and pulling it closed, he said a silent prayer of gratitude to the seamstress who had fitted the dress perfectly without a body to use as a model.

His fingers shook as he tightened the closures, and he reminded himself that in a short time he would have the opportunity to reverse the procedure and reveal his bride's body to his touch.

"Oh, Papa," Cammie said, smoothing her hands down the length of the skirt. "This is the most beautiful dress I have ever seen. I feel like a princess. Thank you, thank you. You are the best papa ever." She wrapped her arms around his neck, and with the assistance of the stool, she was the proper height for their lips to meet for the first time.

Her lips were soft against his and the contact startled Alexander. He had not planned to initiate any sort of touching such as this until after their wedding, not wishing to frighten his wee bride, nor did he trust himself to refrain from plunging ahead much too quickly for an innocent miss such as Cammie. But, when her delicate hands rested upon his chest and her mouth met his, a swirl of warmth and longing spun through him the likes of which he had never experienced before. The kiss, their first kiss, was a gentle affair with Cammie experimenting with the feel of contact between them. Holding himself back as much as possible, he allowed her to lead in this instance and though his lips responded to her touch, he did not intensify the contact.

To his surprise, his diminutive bride-to-be slid her hands from his chest to around his neck and pulled his face closer to hers while she moved her mouth beneath his.

"Damnation, Camellia, how am I to behave when you do such things," he said, pulling away from her and resting his mouth against her forehead.

Cammie stiffened in his embrace and used her hands to push away from him. "I-I am sorry, Papa," she whispered, hanging her head.

~

Cammie could scarce believe the mistake she had made.

She had never kissed a man before and clearly did not know what she was doing, why else would her papa react in such a dramatic manner? Had she behaved like a doxy and shocked and shamed her papa?

She hopped off the stool, rushed into her bedroom and crawled onto the bed, buried her face in the pile of lace pillows and sobbed.

She had no idea where the wave upon wave of sadness came from, but they swept over her in a rush and, before she knew it, she had nearly soaked one of the pillows through. Her nose was running and she sat up to look about for a handkerchief when one magically appeared and she glanced up to see her papa standing over her, sadness and concern etched on his face.

"What is wrong, little Cammie? Did something frighten you?"

She reached for the monogrammed square of linen, but he ignored her movements and sat on the bed next to her, taking her upon his lap and holding the soft fabric to her nose. "Blow," he said and she complied with a noisy honk that made him chuckle. "Good girl."

"Now," he said, situating her upon his lap, "why the tears? Did you not enjoy kissing me?"

"Y-you said a foul word, Papa." She stared at the frilly coverlet of her bed and worked some of the fancywork edging between her fingers. "Oh, Papa. I-I must confess something to you. It is something I have never told anyone before, but I feel I must tell you before you commit yourself to me forever."

Papa's eyebrows shot up and his head tilted to the side, but he quickly composed himself and set her out upon his knee so he could get a proper look at her face. "If you have something important to tell me, Camellia, then I shall give you my full attention." He brushed a wisp of hair away from her face. "What troubles you, my little bride?"

She studied his features and her heart cracked with pain, but she forced herself to confess the thing that had been niggling at her conscience. "Papa," she whispered, "I-I have memories of my mama and...and...I think she was a-a p-prostitute." She said the word and then let out a giant breath she had been holding. "Wh-what if I am like her? I cannot control my urges, even after all the years Miss Wickersham spent making a proper lady out of me."

There was a long pause during which Cammie felt certain her papa was trying to figure out how to get her out of his house as quickly as possible.

Perhaps she ought to have kept quiet, but already she loved her papa too much to let him suffer the shame of her vulgar bloodline.

To her surprise, Papa pulled her close to his chest and buried his face in her hair, then tipped her face up so he could look into her eyes as he spoke. "Thank you for trusting me with your secret. You are a courageous young lady, and I am proud of you for telling me."

Cammie stared into his beautiful dark eyes, memorizing the color and shape in case she never saw him again.

"I am going to tell you something very important," he said, "and you must listen carefully because I never want you to worry about this issue again. All I need to know about your mother, or any of your relations, is that she created you, a beautiful, sweet, desirable young lady who I will be proud to have as my wife, Lady Cavendish, forever. Do you understand?"

Shocked, Cammie gaped at her papa and nodded her head. "Yes, Papa. Are you absolutely certain?"

"I have never been more certain of anything in my life," he said, before taking her lips with his.

CHAPTER 7

It had been a day of greetings and good-byes for Cammie. First thing in the morning she had said good-bye to Hyacinth, Daisy, Rosie and the other girls at Talcott House, even bossy Garland, with a lump in her throat, excited about meeting her papa, but also anxious over leaving the place that had been her home and safe haven for six years. Her life before Talcott House had been filled with hunger and fear. What she could never get over was the freezing cold of winter. Even now, the slightest blast of winter cold filled her with fear and anxiety, a physical reminder of the hardships she had endured. Hardships which Miss Wickersham and now Lord Cavendish had assured her were a thing long in the past. Still, those were memories she might never banish from her thinking.

The sadness of her departure was overshadowed by the thrill of meeting Lord Cavendish, the man who would be her husband and very special papa who would care for her and love her. A thrill of excitement fluttered through her stomach just thinking about it. And then she had said good-bye to Miss Wickersham. Hardly a tear filled departure, as

Miss Wickersham kept a tight rein on her own emotions, but Cammie felt certain she had heard a small catch in her teacher's voice as she said good-bye and wished Cammie happiness in her future. Miss Wickersham might have even wiped away a tear or two during the wedding ceremony which had been conducted in the drawing room with the vicar officiating and Lord Cavendish's manservant and Miss Wickersham as witnesses.

Now, it was afternoon and Cammie's busy day still had much activity left to it. She was officially Lady Cavendish. She stood next to her husband and hugged herself around the middle hardly able to believe the turn her life had taken. She shuddered to think what might have happened to her without the benevolent intervention of Miss Wickersham.

Papa and Cammie were eating their evening meal in his large master bedroom upon a small table that had been set up near the window so they could see the sun lowering in the evening sky as they dined.

Cammie tried to eat her food like a good girl but her attention kept being drawn to the large bed which occupied the majority of the room. Papa's room. The room where he had said they would sleep together and share a bed. Cammie still was not entirely certain what happened between married people in the bed, despite Nurse Lister's explanation, but the jittery feeling in her stomach made it hard for her to eat her dinner.

"Camellia," Papa said, pausing until she met his gaze before he continued, "is there a problem with the food? If so, I will speak to cook about it immediately."

"Oh no, Papa," Cammie replied. She hated the idea of the cook getting a scolding simply because she was too nervous to eat. "The food is delicious."

"If it is so delicious, as you say, Camellia, then why does so much remain upon your plate?" Papa's voice was stern but there was a twinkle in his eye that made Cammie feel not quite so nervous about his question.

"I," she started to answer but her eyes kept wandering to the bed with its heap of pillows and large soft looking quilt. It was so high up from the floor, she wondered if she would even be able to get in and out of it without assistance. Her toes curled in her shoes as she thought about Papa lifting her into the bed.

"I see that you seem preoccupied by the bed, is that true, Cammie?"

If she answered truthfully, would he think she was too forward? However, she dared not lie, not to her papa, not on their wedding day. When she did not answer quickly enough, Papa tapped his finger on the linen covered table. "I am awaiting your reply, Camellia."

"I-I am nervous about...about..." Her eyes darted to the bed again and then back down at the plate of food getting cold on the table before her. "Papa, I do not know what...what I mean to say is...what if you...what if I..."

Papa chuckled and taking her hand in his, gently pulled her from her seat and set her upon his lap. It seemed to be a favorite way for him to hold and talk to her and Cammie had no complaints for she liked it very much too. "It will be for me to teach you the things that married people do together, Cammie. That is my honor and duty as your husband."

Yes, Papa," she replied and snuggled against his strong torso. When she finally relaxed against him, a large yawn pushed its way from her lips. She hurriedly covered it with both her hands and hoped that Papa did not notice, but it seemed her papa saw and heard everything she did and sometimes even what she thought.

"I believe," Papa said, placing a sweet kiss upon her forehead, "that perhaps I need to put my little girl to bed for a nap before we commence our wedding night activities."

Cammie sat up straight. "No, Papa, please. I do not want to wait."

Papa's dark gaze stilled any further protests but also heated up the swirl of desire forming in her nether region. "There will be no contradicting me, Cammie. Do I make myself clear?"

"Yes, Papa. I am sorry." She buried her face in his woolen jacket and wrapped her arms around his waist. "If you believe I need to take a nap, then that is what I shall do."

"That's my good girl," Papa said, setting her on her feet in front of him before he stood and took her hand. Leading her back to the dressing room, he lifted her to stand atop the dressing stool. His eyes raked over her body and then he gazed into her eyes and told her how beautiful she was and how proud he was to have her as his wife. Cammie blushed and thanked him. Gently, he touched her shoulder to indicate his wish for her to turn around so he could open the fastenings on the beautiful white lace dress he had selected for her. Cammie stifled another yawn. Much as she did wish for some sleep, she loathed the idea of shedding the exquisite gown which made her feel like royalty.

Papa pushed the gown down her body and ordered her to step out of the garment. He made quick work of removing her chemise next, but allowed her to keep her drawers on, for which she was grateful. Though she felt comfortable around her papa, being completely unclothed before him still made her flush from head to toe. He turned her around to face him, and she couldn't help but notice the heat in his dark gaze. Her heart fluttered and she beamed with a slight amount of pride, happy that he seemed to like the look of her body. She wasn't as tall or curvy as most women, for which she had sometimes felt self-consciousness. She stole another glance into her caring papa's handsome eyes, yet again thankful for the match Miss Wickersham had made for her.

He held up the prettiest nightdress she'd ever seen, the long sleeves and the bottom of the skirt embroidered with tiny elegant flowers. The soft cotton garment fit her perfectly, and she impulsively did a little spin for Papa once he finished putting it on her, giggling as the skirt flared out in a billowing wave.

Papa chuckled and stepped back, his eyes roving over her body. "I'm pleased you like it, Cammie."

She stifled another yawn. "Thank you, Papa. I love it. It's beautiful, and I feel like a princess right now."

He grasped her hand and led her back into her bedroom. "I hope you feel like a sleepy princess."

"I will try my hardest to sleep for a while, Papa. I promise." Another yawn. Perhaps the excitement of the last few days was finally catching up with her. As he guided her toward the bed, the heaviness of fatigue swept over her. Well, maybe she would fall asleep more easily than she'd originally thought.

And once she woke up…

Her heart raced. Papa would take her into his bedroom. Despite her nervousness and uncertainty about what exactly would happen in Papa's bedroom, she found herself looking forward to this evening more and more.

Papa pulled back the covers and moved the decorative pillows to a nearby chair. Then he picked her up as if she weighed nothing and laid her on the bed. She sighed with pleasure at the feel of the soft sheets and fluffy pillow. While she'd had her own warm bed to sleep in at Talcott House, it was nothing compared to the luxuriousness of this bed. She felt positively spoiled as she ran her fingers over the sheets. She hadn't known it was possible to find linens so soft. Papa had truly spared no expense in furnishing her bedroom. She stretched out as he pulled the thick covers atop her, enjoying the weight of the blankets.

"Thank you, Papa. This is the most comfortable bed ever."

He sat beside her and tucked the covers up to her neck, taking great care to ensure she was snug. She stared up at him, in awe at how protected he made her feel. Nothing could hurt her when Papa was here. He would keep all the monsters away, and he would make sure she was always warm and safe. Her heart swelled with affection for the handsome man she'd met but a few hours ago.

Her new papa. Her new husband. Her whole world.

Her eyes felt heavy and she yawned yet again.

"Sleep tight, my little bride." Papa leaned down to kiss her forehead. He gave her a warm smile and stroked her hair, then walked across the room to close the curtains before departing the room.

A dreamy sigh escaped Cammie's lips. She smiled to herself and closed her eyes, as her increasing weariness pulled her deeper and deeper into the oblivion of sleep. Her last thought before she finally drifted off was that she must be the luckiest little girl in the whole wide world.

~

ALEXANDER PULLED out his pocket watch, and, noting that Cammie had been quiet in her bedroom for over two hours now, decided it was time to wake his little girl up.

His little girl. His heart warmed at the thought. She was his to love, cherish, and guide for the rest of their lives. And, once he awoke her and brought her into his room, they would officially consummate their marriage. Lust spiraled through him and he fought to steady his hand as he opened her door and slipped inside, careful to be quiet and not disturb her from her dreams. He had the strong desire to look upon her as she lay sleeping.

He approached her petite, slumbering form, and stood

above her, staring down at the beautiful sweet girl he was proud to call his wife. She shifted slightly and a soft moan escaped her lips, and it was then that he noticed her hand moving beneath the covers.

"Cammie?" he said, but her eyes remained shut. She was fast asleep, lost in a dream.

A naughty dream, he amended, as he slowly peeled back her covers and sheets to discover her with her nightgown bunched up around her waist and her hand buried between her thighs. She stuck her hand down into her drawers.

A flash of anger hit him, that she would disobey him again so soon, but then he realized she likely couldn't help herself. He could hardly hold her accountable for something that happened while she slept.

His cock leapt and his balls tightened, his breaths coming short and ragged. He watched her for several moments, unable to speak or look away. Another little moan drifted from her.

"Papa," she said in a whisper. "Oh, Papa."

His breath caught in his chest. She was dreaming about him!

He swallowed hard and sat beside her, and waited for her to rouse on her own. The shifting of his weight on the mattress must have disturbed her naughty dreams, because her eyes soon fluttered open and she peered up at him, blinking in confusion. Once the sleep cleared from her gaze, she gave him a small smile.

"Good evening, Papa. Is it still evening?"

"Yes, it's still evening, Cammie. You only slept for two hours. Of course, it looks like you did more than sleep, little girl," he said, keeping his visage playful but hardening his voice.

Her brows knitted together. "What do you mean?"

He nodded at her center, where her hand remained stuck down her drawers, though her fingers had stopped stroking.

"Oh no!" She gasped and tore her hand out of her drawers, then arranged her nightdress about her in frantic movements, trying to cover herself. "Papa! I didn't mean to!" She grabbed for the covers next, but he placed his hands on her shoulders, forcing her to still.

"Cammie, look at me."

Worried eyes met his. "Oh, Papa, I am so sorry."

"Cammie, I want you to be a good girl and lay back. Keep your legs spread."

She obeyed, though the nervousness didn't leave her expression. It pleased him that she acquiesced to his demands so quickly, even though she hadn't meant to break a rule.

He pushed her skirt up and reached for the ties on her drawers, unfastening them and yanking the undergarment down. He tossed her drawers onto the same chair as the pillows and turned back to gaze upon her sweet little cunny. His cock swelled harder, his anticipation over their wedding night growing. He couldn't wait to kiss every inch of her body and then slowly push his hardness into her tight virgin cunny, breaking her in and making her his wife-in-truth.

She was all smooth and pink, and he noticed a glimmer of moisture peeking out from her slightly parted folds.

"You're such a good girl for spreading your legs so wide for your papa."

She flushed. "Th-thank you, Papa. Are yo-you going to spank my kitty now because I was naughty?" She bit her lower lip and peered up at him imploringly.

He cupped her warm mound and lifted an eyebrow at her. "As long as you confess to Papa what you were dreaming about, you will only receive five light smacks. Unless, of course, you prove uncooperative while I administer those five smacks. Little girls who can't keep their legs spread for their papas get extra punishment. Now, what were you dreaming of?"

"Well, Papa," she said, her nervous countenance breaking into an intense look of concentration, "I was dreaming about you touching me. Dreaming about you sliding your fingers in and out of my kitty. And, you also kissed me until I could scarcely breathe."

"I see. Thank you for telling me." He waited until her gaze returned to his. "Now, remember, you will keep your legs spread wide during your punishment. You don't want Papa to have to give you extra slaps to your smooth little kitty lips, do you?"

"I'll hold still, Papa. I don't want any extras." She clutched the sheets beneath her and took a deep breath in anticipation of the first smack.

Alexander lifted his hand and brought it down lightly atop her folds, centering the brunt of the slap over her protruding nubbin. She gasped and arched her back, and her legs trembled as she gasped for air. He smacked her again.

"Naughty." Another slap. "How dare you touch what belongs to your papa? Naughty, naughty, naughty." He delivered the final three smacks in quick succession, but forced her to keep her legs spread once her punishment was over.

A copious amount of moisture glistened atop her reddened folds. Alexander became dizzy for a moment as all the blood in his body rushed south. Then he swept her up into his arms and carried her into his bedroom.

He had to have her now.

CHAPTER 8

Alexander sat Cammie on her feet just long enough to pull her nightdress over her head. He tossed it aside and lifted her up onto his bed, forcing her to lay back and spread her thighs for him yet again. He took a steadying breath and reached for her cunny, delving two fingers into her core, until he met the resistance of her virginal barrier. Keeping his digits submerged, he placed his thumb atop her swollen nub and circled it with increasing pressure.

"Papa!" She jerked against him, gyrating wantonly against his hand.

"How does this compare to your dream, little one?" he asked, leaning down to kiss her.

Their lips met in a tender joining at first, but when she moaned against his mouth, he lost all control and deepened the kiss, taking command and not breaking contact until she squealed. Realizing she needed air, he withdrew and stared down at her, pressing harder on her nubbin as he swirled. Her eyes fluttered shut and she twisted around, so beautifully responsive to his touch.

"This is better than my dream, Papa. Much better," she whispered.

He stroked her quim for another moment, and with great reluctance, pulled his hand from her center. If he was going to claim her, he had to get his blasted clothing off first. He crawled off the bed and hastily undressed. He shed his trousers and stockings, and then worked open his neckcloth, his gaze intent on his little bride. She watched him with wide eyes that kept trailing to his rigid cock. He tossed his neckcloth and shirt to the floor, his need for her burgeoning to new heights. Once he crawled into bed, they would be skin to skin.

"Papa?" She sounded worried.

"Yes, my love?"

"Is that...is that a penis?" Her eyes went even wider as she stared open mouthed at his erect manhood.

"Yes, little one. It's also called a cock." He decided she didn't need to know any other names for the appendage between his legs, though he could have easily come up with a dozen more slang terms. He preferred to keep her innocent.

He wasted no time in getting back into bed, settling atop Cammie with his length pressing at her moist center. He dragged his cock up and down her wet slit, delighting in her whimpers and moans.

"Papa, I don't think it will fit." She stilled and peered down the length of her stomach at his hardness. "It's so big, Papa."

"I assure you, it will fit. It may hurt for a moment, but only this first time. But know that if I could take the pain on myself, I would gladly do so." And he meant it. Yes, he had spanked her and brought her to tears already today, but this particular pain was one he wished he could spare her. Of course, it couldn't be helped, and he endeavored to make it as pleasant as possible. "Trust Papa, Cammie. Once my cock is buried deep in your little cunny, all the tingling and all the aching you've been feeling will soon get better."

"Very well. I-I trust you, Papa," she said, nodding and offering him a brief but reassuring smile.

Her surrender and her trust were the sweetest gifts.

He cupped her breasts, enjoying the weight of them in his hands, and leaned down to capture one nipple in his mouth. He laved at the ripe peak and reached one hand around her to squeeze her bottom. She gasped and writhed underneath him, and he soon paid the same attention to her other nipple, even going so far as to take it between his teeth and tug until she cried out and lifted her center hard against him, as if to compel him to thrust deep into her cunny.

He resisted the urge to drive into her just yet, instead wanting to caress and kiss her all over. He pressed another kiss to her mouth, this one quicker than the last, and moved down her slight form, licking the hollow between her breasts and dragging his teeth over her stomach. He ran his hands over every inch of her body, exploring her in all her perfection. He kept tasting her, too, licking and biting whatever part of her it pleased him to nibble on.

When, finally, he could stand the anticipation no more, he once again settled himself between her thighs. He met her gaze and started a slow push inside her. Holy God, she was tighter than he'd imagined. Her warmth was a vise around his cock, hugging him and drawing him to thrust deeper and deeper, until the tip of his length met resistance. He gathered her hands in one of his, pinning her down beneath him.

Then he drove the rest of the way inside her in one quick hard thrust, pausing once he was fully submerged. She pressed her eyes shut and winced, but only seconds later, she moved enticingly against him, wiggling her hips and struggling as if to free her wrists. But he didn't let her go. He tightened his hold and withdrew from her cunny slightly, only to drive back in with another rapid stroke. And another, and another. He claimed her with abandon, unable to hold back the fire of his passion any longer.

Moments later, he released her wrists and gripped her hips, increasing the pace of his claiming. She clutched the covers until her knuckles turned white. The sound of flesh slapping flesh filled the room, and the scent of her feminine arousal hung heavily in the air. He inhaled deeply, unable to get enough of her.

This, this little girl was his forever. He could hardly fathom it.

The walls of her cunny suddenly tightened around him, and she moaned and jerked her hips up and down, riding the waves of her release. Her breasts bounced with her movements, and her expression was one of pure ecstasy. He followed her soon after, as his vision clouded and he erupted within her. He emptied himself inside her, filling her with his seed.

After he caught his breath, he carefully withdrew his length and gathered her up in his arms. She nestled her head on his chest and gave a sweet sigh, running her fingers in lazy circles over his flesh. He pulled the covers overtop her and their legs entwined together beneath the sheets, and he smoothed her tangled hair from her face and placed a soft kiss to her forehead, the need to take care of her in the aftermath of their first lovemaking overwhelming.

Thunder rumbled in the distance, and not long after the wind howled and rain began pattering the roof as an evening storm swept across London. But the outside world soon faded and it seemed they were the last two people left on the earth. Two hearts beating as one. Husband and wife. Papa and little girl. And, God, did he love her. More than she could possibly ever understand.

~

CAMMIE SAT across from Papa in the dining room, back straight with her hands folded in her lap, while two servants placed platters of toast, jams, fruits, boiled eggs, and baked ham on the table for breakfast. Her stomach rumbled so loudly that Papa smirked and said, "I believe a certain young lady has worked up an appetite this morning."

The servants, bless them, exited the dining room hastily, leaving her alone with her papa. She flushed and glanced away, suddenly shy, despite all the intimacies they had shared the night prior and earlier this morning.

She licked her lips, still tasting the salty tang of Papa's seed on her mouth. She'd never imagined he would require her to suck on his manhood, but he'd pushed her to her knees in his bedroom only an hour ago and ordered her to please him with her mouth.

Though it had been a clumsy affair at first, she had eventually gotten the gist of it, and he helped her by providing proper instruction. His words came back, making her feel faint and causing her kitty to pulse with need.

Hollow your mouth out and open your throat as much as possible.

Let Papa deep into your mouth. Good girl. Just like that.

All your holes belong to your papa. Your cunny. Your mouth. And even your rosebud. Whichever hole I want to fill, that's the hole you will take my cock in, little girl.

"Cammie?"

She looked up from her plate, realizing she had reached for a piece of toast but had not taken a bite yet, let alone covered it with jam or butter. Had Papa been speaking to her? Oh no, she had gotten lost in her thoughts again. She hoped Papa wasn't angry.

"Cammie, did you hear me?"

"Um, sorry, Papa. What did you say?"

"I asked if you would like to go for a walk in the gardens after breakfast? The rain appears to have cleared."

"Of course, Papa. I would be delighted."

She spread a liberal amount of blackberry jam on her toast and took a bite, practically moaning at the tart sweetness. Though she'd never gone hungry at Talcott House, porridge was usually served for breakfast on most mornings. Jam and toast and baked ham were her favorites, and she shoved several bites into her mouth and chewed vigorously.

"Cammie, slow down or you're going to choke."

She finally swallowed and looked at Papa. "I am fine."

"I know for a fact that you have better table manners than that. Now, put your napkin on your lap and take slow, and smaller bites. If I have to tell you again, there will be consequences. The kind that involve you taking a trip over my knee, where you'll get your tiny bare bottom smacked good and hard."

Oh, there it was again. The sharp tingle. The incessant aching.

Why did Papa's threats make her so breathless with what she was beginning to realize was desire? She didn't enjoy the pain of a spanking, but when Papa got stern with her, she couldn't help but flush and squirm in her chair.

With an internal sigh, she sat her toast down and obeyed, placing her napkin over her lap and sitting straighter, exactly how a lady ought to sit at the breakfast table with her handsome lord of a husband.

"Sorry, Papa. It's just all so delicious." She dabbed her lips with her napkin, then replaced it on her lap.

"That's much better. Good girl."

They finished breakfast a while later, with no more instances of bad table manners, and escaped out a back door for a leisurely stroll in the vast gardens of Ashton Manor.

She walked arm in arm with Papa, and she was delighted when he insisted on holding her parasol over her head for her, to help shield her from the bright sun. Water droplets sparkled on some of the flowers and plants in the garden, but the paths that wound through the greenery were mostly dry, and the day was pleasantly warm.

He gave her a brief history of the manor, and told her a little about his parents, both of whom had died not long after he had reached adulthood. Her heart panged for his loss, and she squeezed his hand and willed him to continue, but he kept his emotions guarded and didn't say much more about them, other than that his mother had loved these gardens, and his father had been a man of few words. Still, she got the sense that he had loved them.

She remembered loving her mother, but always being scared of her moods and the strange men who would come to visit on occasion. She recalled sitting by her mother's bedside when she had a fever, and her brother, Robert, telling her that everything would be all right. But it wasn't all right. Her mama had gone to sleep and never woken up. Her next memories were of being cold and hungry on the street. And afraid. So afraid.

She gave her head a shake, trying to banish the dark memories from her thoughts. She was safe now. She had Papa. He wouldn't let her go hungry or freeze. He'd spoiled her with a bedroom filled with clothing and toys. He'd made her feel wanted, and every time he looked at her, her heart did a little dance. She had never been so happy in her life. She felt as if she were floating in the clouds above.

Papa guided her to a sparkling fountain and they sat down along the edge. He clasped her hand and stared into her eyes, and she was so overcome by the level of warmth and affection reflected in his gaze that her throat started to burn. He gave her a smile and she melted on the spot.

"The gardens are more beautiful than I could have ever imagined, Papa. Thank you for showing them to me. And thank you for spending time with me this morning."

"Where else would I be this morning, little one?"

She thought for a moment, worrying her lower lip. "Well, papas have to work a lot. That's what my friend Cynny told me. She said her father—her real father, that is—worked all the time before he passed away and that she hardly ever saw him."

He stroked a hand down her cheek and drew her closer, until she was almost seated in his lap. "I'm a lord and have people who depend on me, so yes, I will have to work. But you are the most important person in my life. You will come first, Cammie, before all others. I swear it. But," he continued, "if you ever start to feel neglected or lonely, I want you to promise me something."

"Promise what?"

"Promise you will come and tell me how you are feeling. I would much rather you tell me how you're feeling, instead of you acting up and getting into mischief just to get my attention. I don't think I need to remind you of what happens to naughty little girls in this household, do I?"

"I understand, and I-I promise, Papa."

He kissed her cheek and she leaned into his show of affection, reveling in the soft warmth of his lips against her skin, and the slight scratch of his whiskers, as he hadn't shaved today. She leaned back and peered at him, admiring how darkly handsome and rugged he looked.

The tingles and aching started to get worse, and she couldn't help but squirm.

Papa gave her a knowing look.

"I think it's time for a bath, young lady. If you're a very good girl for Papa while he bathes you, I'll stroke your kitty and help the aching between your thighs to feel better."

She felt her eyes go wide. "Papa! How do you know about the aching?"

"You keep flushing and fidgeting. I bet your drawers are soaking wet right now, little girl. Come, let's go back inside. Papa's going to give you a thorough bath."

CHAPTER 9

A thorough bath, indeed.

Cammie trembled in the warm water, as she held position on her hands and knees with her bottom jutted up in the air so Papa could properly wash her. She was so embarrassed that he was cleaning her private parts, but she knew if she argued or resisted, he would only spank her bare, wet bottom. The last thing she wanted was another punishment, when her behind still smarted from yesterday's spanking. She didn't want to find out how hard Papa would spank her if she did something especially naughty, and she endeavored to try her best to follow his rules.

"A papa gives his little girl rules because he cares about her," he'd told her right before he'd stripped off her morning gown and ordered her into the tub, which the servants had filled with the perfect temperature of hot water.

The tub was in her bedroom, and the curtains were wide open, the sun illuminating her nakedness. Papa dragged a soapy wet cloth over her kitty, then dipped it into the water and commenced giving her bottom the same careful attention. He'd already washed the rest of her, and he said this was the last, but most important, part of cleaning his little girl.

His touch was making her increasingly hot and achy though. Oh, how she longed for him to caress her kitty again, if only for a few moments. A couple of rubs to her sensitive nubbin, and she felt certain she would soar to the clouds. *Touch me,* she thought. *Please, Papa.*

He answered her unspoken wish, but he didn't caress the part of her she'd wanted. Instead, he pressed a finger against her bum hole. She jerked forward in the tub, sloshing the water around as she attempted to evade his ministrations. That didn't make him happy, and he gave her two hard swats, one to each cheek.

"Ouch! Ouchie! Papa, that hurts!"

"You were naughty. I told you to remain still, little girl. Now, do you remember what I told you this morning, about all your holes belonging to me?"

Oh no. No no no. Not in her bottom hole!

She swallowed hard and finally answered. "Yes, I remember, Papa. But could you please touch my cunny instead?"

Another smack. "What did I say about calling your privates your cunny? Are you a big girl or a little girl, Cammie?"

"I-I'm a little girl. I'm *your* little girl, and you told me not to use a grown up word like that. Sorry, Papa."

He grabbed a towel and wiped up the water from the floor, and she gave him her best apologetic look. She hadn't meant to make a mess. Would he spank her more? She scrambled back into position, on her hands and knees with her bottom lifted high, in hopes that her compliance would please him.

"I better not hear you using language like that again, Cammie. Not only will you end up with a sore bottom, I'll wash your mouth out with soap as well."

She shuddered and resolved to erase every naughty word from her mind. Not long after she'd turned eighteen, she'd gone through a phase at Talcott House during which she'd taken to using bad language, in an effort to impress her friends. Miss Wickersham, however, had not been impressed, and Cammie had had her mouth soaped out several times by her no-nonsense guardian. She made a sour face in remembrance and then nodded in agreement.

"I understand, Papa."

"Good. Now, keep still while I tend to your bottom hole. I wish to see just how tight it is, so I know how much training you will require."

Training? Oh dear. That sounded rather ominous. She tensed up, but that didn't stop him from prying her cheeks apart and pressing at her snug entrance.

"Be a good girl and relax. Let Papa inside."

She glanced over at him, and his kind tone coupled with his encouraging expression prompted her to relax her bottom and put her trust in him. She inhaled and then breathed out slowly, willing herself to calm and soften up enough to allow her papa to more easily breach her back hole.

He swirled a finger around her private entrance and in the next instant, commenced a gradual push into her tightness. Every few seconds, he paused and offered her encouragement, calling her a good girl and praising her for holding still. Finally, when she thought he couldn't possibly push any further, he stopped.

"I'm all the way inside you now. Your little bottom hole is very tight, Cammie."

She whimpered, unable to offer a verbal response.

"Soon I will claim you here with my cock."

Her head jerked up, but she held position otherwise, and

his digit remained buried in her snug hole. “But, Papa! You’re too big. It will never fit!”

He chuckled and his eyes darkened. “I assure you, with the proper training, it won’t be long before I’m pounding into your bottom with my cock.”

Her stomach flipped, but his words and the mental vision of Papa ramming his hugeness into her behind made her kitty clench up, and her breasts began to ache as if calling out for his touch. Would she like it when Papa stuck his cock in her bottom hole? Her face heated as she imagined getting onto her hands and knees on his bed and offering her most secret entrance to him.

How would he train her to accept his cock? Would he stick his fingers in her bottom during her bath time every day? She cast another glance at him and realized that beneath the fullness and slight discomfort of having her rosebud violated, there was a part of her that wanted more. Wanted him to add another finger, or thrust his digit in and out. She took a shaky breath and returned her stare to the soapy water.

Oh how she hoped Papa took her to his bedroom soon. If he didn’t make the aching go away, she would surely combust or lose control and start to think about touching herself.

To her delight, he dried her off and led her, stark naked, into his masculine room. Despite her nudity, she wasn’t cold. The heat of the nearby braziers wafted across her flesh. Papa kissed her and caressed her all over, leaving her breathless with anticipation. When he stripped his clothes off and crawled under the covers with her, the intimate contact of skin on skin warmed her further.

“You’re so beautiful, Cammie. So perfect.”

“Thank you, Papa,” she said shyly. “I think you’re perfect too.”

They spent the afternoon in his bed. He took her over and over again, with only brief pauses in between, during which he held her close and they talked of inconsequential things, everything from their favorite musical compositions to their favorite time of year. She preferred the summer months, while he enjoyed winter.

"The only thing more beautiful than a landscape covered in freshly fallen snow is you, my sweet Cammie," he said before crawling atop her again.

She parted her thighs and surrendered.

She was and always would be his for the taking.

CHAPTER 10

Cammie glanced out the carriage windows at the streets of London. This was her first outing with Papa since their marriage. It seemed everything appeared much different to Cammie now that she was a married lady. Lady Cavendish to be exact. A shiver of excitement ran through her tummy and her toes wiggled in her shoes at the mere thought that she was indeed Lady Cavendish, now and forever. A small flush warmed her cheeks as she remembered all of the ways Papa had claimed her. Yes, she was well and truly his.

The view from the Cavendish family carriage as it rolled through the streets of Mayfair and the other prosperous neighborhoods of the city contrasted dramatically with what she remembered of the dank, dreary tenement section of town where she and her brother, Robert, had tried to scrape out an existence. So many years had gone by since then, it was hard for Cammie to even believe that period had been part of her life.

She peeked out the corner of her eye at the handsome man who was her husband and her papa. She could scarcely fathom the grand turn her life had taken. Married just over a week, Cammie had found herself happier than she ever imagined she could be. Fulfilled, satisfied, loved and cared for and all of this because of her papa. Oh, she supposed if she was really going back to the whole source of her life's change in course, Miss Wickersham deserved the credit.

Now that Cammie was a little older and wiser in the ways of the world, or so she believed after a week of marital bliss, the realization of what might have happened to her had her brother been successful in his plan to hire her out as a scullery maid to a family known to be cruel and abusive with their servants—not that Robert realized it at the time—she did not blame him for it, but her life would have been drastically different.

She glanced down at her hands encased in a new pair of gloves with her monogram CC for Camellia Cavendish embroidered into the leather on the inner wrist of each glove and thought about what her hands might look like if she had spent the last six years working as a scullery maid rather than her current circumstance of sitting perched inside a luxurious carriage emblazoned with the Cavendish family crest. She now had a family. She belonged.

"What are you thinking about, little Cammie?" Papa asked.

"I am thinking about all you have been teaching me," she said with a blush. "I had no idea of the things that married people did together," she said. "Thank you for being such a patient teacher."

"And thank you for being such a willing pupil." Papa caressed her cheek. "In fact, that is why we are off to Mrs. Stilton's Milliner shop today. I would like to get you a present to thank you and to honor you for being such a good wife."

"Thank you, Papa, but you do not need to buy me hats for me to love you more."

"But a new hat will not cause you to love me any less, will it, my dear?"

"Papa! You make it sound bad," Cammie said with a laugh, her love for him growing every minute.

"You look very pretty today, my Cammie," her papa said giving her a warm smile and squeezing her hand.

"Thank you, Papa," she said. "You chose a particularly pretty dress for me today and I thank you for that."

"It is one of my great delights to dress you each morning, my dear," Papa said then winked. "Though it is second only to the great delight I take in undressing you."

"Papa!" Cammie exclaimed. "You make me blush."

"I enjoy making you blush. I enjoy everything with you, my sweet Cammie." The affection in his eyes filled Cammie with awe. She never knew it was possible to be loved so thoroughly and completely.

"You are the best papa in the whole wide world and I thank you for everything you do for me. Are you sure that we need to go shopping for a new hat? The one that I'm wearing now is even more beautiful than the one I wore yesterday which is more beautiful than the one I wore the day before that."

"Well, there's always tomorrow then the day after tomorrow and the day after that and you will need beautiful hats for each of those days, my darling Cammie, and I shall make sure that you have them."

Cammie looked up at her papa and said, "Are you certain, dear papa that your desire to have me properly hatted is not the result of your less-than-stellar talent at arranging my hair?" Cammie gave him a saucy look while holding back a giggle.

Quick as a flash, Papa had Cammie over his lap and

administered five swift swats to her bottom and placed her back in her seat before she knew what had happened to her. "You are lucky, little Cammie, that we are not at home in your dressing room right now because I would use the hair-brush on you. That seems the appropriate punishment for someone who mocks my efforts at styling your beautiful hair."

The giggle she had been holding back burst from Cammie's lips. "Papa," she said, "you are being very silly, though I must admit your skills are vastly improving."

"It would seem, my dear," Papa said, "that we are both teaching each other new things, are we not?" The meaning of his words and the look he gave her started slow heat burning through Cammie. Her face flushed and her kitty began to feel warm and tingly like it did so often when she was in her Papa's presence.

"Papa!" Cammie exclaimed blushing and glancing about the interior of the carriage as though someone might hear them. "What a scandalous thing to say in public."

"We are not in public." And to prove his point, he slid his hand inside the bodice of her dress and cupped her breast while he continued to speak, the brush of his thumb over her ninny making it difficult for Cammie to concentrate on his words. "The only ones who might hear are the servants. My staff has been well trained, Camellia. Anything they see or hear they will keep private or they will find themselves off looking for a new job and well they know it."

"Besides," he said, giving her a lengthy glance from head to toe while he continued to fondle her breast, "it is no secret that I adore you and surely the staff is well aware of that, if not from your moans of pleasure, then possibly from your squeals when you are disciplined."

"Papa," Cammie gasped. The mere mention of her husband's firm discipline, combined with the naughty sensations he stimulated in her breast made her lightheaded. "I really must insist. We are in public, people can see in the windows."

Papa gave her a stern look as well as a particularly hard pinch to her nipple. "You must insist?" he asked, rolling the tip of her breast between his thumb and forefinger until she moaned and swayed in his direction. "Tell me, Camellia," he asked, his voice a husky whisper, "who is in charge of you, body and soul?" The bodice of her dress was pushed to the side and his mouth took over where his fingers had been.

"P-papa, no," she gasped again and tried to pull away. "You cannot do that."

To her great relief, Papa raised his head from her breast, though the sight of her exposed nipple slick from Papa's lips and tongue gave her the squirmies and part of her dearly wished he would continue.

Her relief was short-lived, however, because Papa gave her breast two quick slaps. "No? Did you just tell your papa no?"

"I would hate for us to be late for our appointment with Mrs. Stilton," she said, hoping Papa's penchant for punctuality would ward off further embarrassment.

Papa gave her a stern look. "The carriage moves at the same pace, regardless of whether I am enjoying the bounty of my wife's body or not."

Cammie had the squirmies again, but this time for a different reason. That look in Papa's eyes did not bode well for her backside. And they were having such a lovely outing too. Had she spoiled everything? But, how could a proper lady travel about the city in the middle of the day with her bare breast out where anyone could see? She explained her concerns to Papa. In response, he pulled down the other side of her bodice and gave her other globe two swift slaps before gathering both of her aching breasts in his hands and burying his face between them, his fingers and mouth working her into a frenzy.

Cammie's head fell back against the upholstered seat, and she buried her hands in his hair. She ought to resist, she told herself, but it felt too good.

While he suckled her right breast, he used his free hand to reach below the skirts of her dress. Cammie gave a half-hearted moan of protest which was met with a slap to her kitty. "Cammie, your objections make me feel as though you do not trust me to know what is best for you," he said before moving to tug at the peak of her other breast with his teeth.

"B-but, Papa, I do trust you." Her voice came out ragged, his fingers in her kitty sending pulses of desire through her body.

"Then I would suggest you quit objecting and enjoy the climax Papa is about to give you."

"No, Papa," she said, as the waves of desire built and churned through her. "You know I make such loud and unladylike noises when I c-come." She gasped as his fingers tugged at the nubbin at the top of her kitty.

"I know," he said, taking one of her hands and pressing it to his cock. "I want you to feel how hard my cock gets when I hear your moans of pleasure."

Even through the leather of her gloves and the fabric of his trousers, Papa's desire for her was evident. She licked her lips, remembering the feel of his hard member between her lips.

"Papa," she said, "I am about to c-climax." Turning her face, she tried to muffle her sex sounds in the fabric of the carriage seat.

"Cammie," Papa's voice was hoarse, "do not turn away. Look at me. I want to watch you come, little wife."

With a load moan that surely was heard by the footmen

and drivers, if not the pedestrians on the sidewalks, Cammie exploded in a climax that left her panting and weak.

"Remember, in public you must address me as *Lord Cavendish*, or simply as *my lord*," Papa said, righting her skirts and bodice. "Perhaps we will take care of my needs on the ride home." Cammie noticed that his fingers were unsteady at the task and she smiled knowing she affected him as much as he affected her.

Before she could reply, and protest his suggestion that they engage in more carnal activities on the way home, the carriage stopped and a footman sprung into action opening the door for them. Papa exited first and waved the footman out of the way as he offered his hand to his bride and assisted her in descending from the carriage. Cammie's face flushed and she kept her gaze away from the footmen, certain they had heard her cries of ecstasy.

Papa said a few words to the driver and then escorted his wife into the milliner's shop.

Cammie gasped. Until this time all of her clothing had been provided for her and selected by others. Before Miss Wickersham, of course, she'd had very little clothing and certainly none of it had ever been made especially for her. Mostly what she wore were scraps and hand-me-downs and rags. When she arrived at Talcott House, there were clothes, but the garments were issued by Miss Wickersham. It was not unusual for them to have been remade from one of the older girls. Cammie was not so foolish or vain as to think Miss Wickersham should have provided a brand new wardrobe for each of her girls. All of that gave her an extra appreciation for the beautiful gowns, day dresses, hats, gloves, capes, boots, stockings and naughty undergarments which her papa had selected especially for her.

And now they had entered the most glorious haven of hats she had ever imagined in her entire life. She couldn't wait to tell her dear friend Cynny, who had recently written to inform Cammie she would soon have a papa of her very own, all about this marvelous shop in her next letter. Hats of every style and color adorned the walls and an elegant woman rushed toward them. "Hello, Lord Cavendish," she said. "How pleased I am to see you this morning."

"Mrs. Stilton," Papa said, taking Cammie's hand and drawing her forward. "May I present my new bride, Lady Cavendish."

Cammie's heart swelled with pride hearing her papa refer to her as his bride, Lady Cavendish. Mrs. Stilton bobbed a curtsy to Cammie. "Welcome to my shop, Lady Cavendish," she said. "I am honored to have you here and I hope that I can serve your needs."

"You have a lovely assortment of hats and other items, Mrs. Stilton," Papa said. "I think I would like to see Lady Cavendish in something in a pale blue to bring out the color in her eyes. Do you have anything that might suit?"

"Oh, most certainly I do, Lord Cavendish. Please Lord Cavendish, Lady Cavendish, won't you step this way?" Mrs. Stilton escorted them to an area near the back of the shop with several large mirrors and a cozy padded seat that she pulled away from a dressing table so Cammie could sit down. "If you will simply wait here for just a moment I have several hats I think will be to your liking and I will bring them for you to try on."

"If you do not mind," Lord Cavendish said to Mrs. Stilton in a tone Cammie knew meant that whether Lady Stilton minded or not, Lord Cavendish would have his way, "I should like to select the hats myself. Perhaps you can come along and help me to bring them back here while Lady Cavendish waits."

"Oh yes, of course, of course, Lord Cavendish. I would be happy to assist you in that way." She rang a bell and a young lady of about Cammie's age emerged from the back of the shop.

"Priscilla," she directed, "please see to Lady Cavendish's needs while I assist Lord Cavendish."

"Yes, ma'am." Priscilla acknowledged her employer before turning to Cammie. "My lady, may I bring you a cup of tea or other refreshments?"

It took a moment for Cammie to realize the young woman was talking to her. After years in seclusion at Talcott House, Cammie was unaccustomed to being in a shop and having someone her own age wait upon her.

"No, thank you." Cammie smiled at Priscilla. She reminded her of Hyacinth and suddenly Cammie felt lonely for a friend. "It must be nice to work in a shop like this."

Priscilla appeared taken aback. Cammie had likely overstepped a boundary by engaging the employee in chit chat. "Y-yes," she said, "it is good to have a job, and I am glad I did not have to go into household service."

"Yes, I would much prefer to work here too," Cammie said.

"My lady, please forgive my forwardness, but I do not believe common employment is a concern for the wife of Lord Cavendish."

Cammie flushed. "I am new to life as Lady Cavendish," she said. "Sometimes I forget."

Priscilla's brows furrowed. Fearing she had shared too much, Cammie changed the subject. "Are you married?" she asked.

Priscilla blushed and glanced at the floor. "No," she said, pausing as though debating whether to say more. "But," she added, "there is a young man who makes deliveries here. We sometimes walk out together on Sunday afternoons. We are both working hard to save money so we can afford to get married, but after expenses, there is not much left over for either of us. Well, if he were to ask, that is..." Her voice drifted off and her face turned pink.

"Oh." Cammie perked up. "How exciting. Please tell me more about him."

"No, my lady, it is not proper. I have said too much already. No one is interested in me."

"I am," Cammie said. "It is a wonderfully romantic story."

A bell at the back door signaled a delivery and Priscilla's eyes lit up. "I must go," she said with an excited smile.

"I hope it is him." Cammie was nearly as excited as the shopgirl. She watched as Priscilla patted her hair and hurried to the delivery door. She would give anything to take a look at the young man who made her new friend blush so prettily. Glancing toward the front of the shop, she saw Papa pass a hat to Mrs. Stilton whose hands were already full. They would return soon. She dared not move from her seat. A shiver ran up her spine remembering how Papa had punished her when they first met and she had wandered into the garden without permission. Her little kitty, already swollen and eager from the interlude in the carriage, quivered with the recollection.

The voices of Priscilla and the delivery man wafted in Cammie's direction. The young man laughed and the sound of it triggered another memory, this one much further into the recesses of her brain. No, it could not be, she told herself, then turned to the mirror to examine her flushed cheeks. A fleeting reflection in the corner of the mirror caught her attention. With a gasp she swung around and charged toward the back of the shop, Papa and his rules forgotten.

She moved past a display of gloves, bumping half of them to the floor in her haste, and could just make out the delivery man's profile. Robert. A flood of emotions swirled through her at the sight of her brother after so many years. He had grown to manhood, but she recognized the familiar features.

Opening her mouth to call out to him, her movements were halted by a firm hand upon her upper arm.

"Camellia," Papa's breath warmed her ear, his voice low in warning, "did I or did I not instruct you to remain seated?"

Gaping up at her Papa, Cammie heard the bell above the back door jingle and knew her brother had left. Her eyes moved to try to catch a glimpse of him but Papa's fingers closed more tightly on her arm. "I expect you to look at me when I am talking to you, Cammie. Have you forgotten the rules so quickly? And just look at the mess you've made. You ought to be ashamed of yourself, young lady."

Her heart sank. Not only had she missed her opportunity to speak to Robert, she had broken one of Papa's rules, not to mention made quite a scene in the shop. Her bottom tingled, anticipating Papa's reaction to her misbehavior.

"I am sorry, my lord," she said, staring at the floor as Priscilla cleaned up the toppled gloves.

Papa did not reply. Disappointment emanated from him and Cammie hated herself for not living up to his expectations.

Glancing past Papa's shoulder, she saw Mrs. Stilton arranging half a dozen exquisite hats near the area where Cammie ought to have been.

Continuing his grip on her arm, Papa signaled Priscilla with his other hand and the shopgirl immediately responded, having quickly fixed the display of gloves. "Yes, my lord. How may I help you?"

"Thank you for cleaning up the gloves. Now, I have some business to attend to with Mrs. Stilton," he said. "I would appreciate it if you would make certain my wife does not move from this spot. Not one inch."

Shamed, Cammie stared at the floor, embarrassment flaming her cheeks.

"Y-yes, my lord," Priscilla said. "I will."

"See that you do." Papa turned sharply on his heel and left the two of them alone.

A single tear fell from Cammie's eye and dripped upon the floor. A worn handkerchief appeared in her line of sight. "Thank you," she whispered, dabbing at her eye.

"Do not feel badly," Priscilla said. "You are not the first woman whose husband has chastised her over something that happened here. You should have seen the row last week when a new bride told her husband to mind his business. He took her outside, leaned her over the hitching post and spanked her bottom. Right there. In broad daylight."

Priscilla's tale distracted Cammie sufficiently from her own misery and she looked up at her new friend. "Even I know better than to do something like that."

The two girls giggled softly for a moment.

"Was that the delivery man you told me about?" Cammie asked.

Priscilla blushed. "Yes. His name is Robert."

Cammie's pulse pounded in her ears, but she forced herself to remain calm. "How often does he make deliveries here?"

"He told me he would return at this time on Friday," Priscilla said, a smile spreading across her mouth.

Friday. Just three days away.

CHAPTER 11

Alexander poured himself a glass of sherry from the decanter on the desk in his library and reflected on events of the day.

The morning had not gone as he had planned. He had awoken with high expectations of the morning. First, to take his dear wife, Cammie, shopping for some new hats and other accessories at the shop run by Mrs. Stilton. He also intended to purchase some items from the back room of Mrs. Stilton's store, an area known only to a small group of patrons. Mrs. Stilton was a woman wise in business as well as the ways of the world and she supplemented her income substantially with those items which she carried in the back room, the key to which was closely guarded by Mrs. Stilton.

Rather than the pleasure of seeing his young bride's face light up with the new hats that he purchased for her followed by a surprise stop at the ice cream store as a special treat since she had told him she had never tried the fashionable dessert, instead they had ridden home with an awkward silence hanging between them for the first time in their marriage. When he had returned from his trip to the back room with Mrs. Stilton, he was pleased, somewhat, to find that Cammie had obediently stayed with the shop girl. At least she had not turned into a completely undisciplined wife. But, rather than continuing their appointment to try on hats, he had made their apologies to Mrs. Stilton and escorted his surprised wife out of the store and back into the carriage without making a purchase other than the one which he had made himself from the back room.

His plan had originally also included a trip to a conservatory for a concert that afternoon. Cammie was particularly fond of music and he wished to lavish her with delights for her body and soul.

Instead his wife was now bent over the edge of the sofa in his library naked, holding her bottom cheeks apart exposing her little rosebud for his view and punishment.

"Oh, Papa," Cammie said, her face pressed against the fabric of the arm of the sofa. "I am so very sorry that I did not obey you and wait where you wanted me to stay while we were at Mrs. Stilton's shop."

"If you knew what you were supposed to do, my dear, then why did you disobey?"

"I-I do not know, Papa," she wailed in misery and his heart squeezed with emotion for his misbehaving but still adorable bride.

However, he could not allow his emotions to soften his resolve. She had behaved badly and failed to follow a simple request. He had not been away from her for more than a few minutes. Why did she not comply?

He was particularly disappointed in her failure to disclose her reasoning. Though not a man who tolerated excuses, he was always willing to listen to some reasonable explanation for his wife's, or anyone else's, misdeeds. When she offered none, he found it rather confusing and surprising. It was uncharacteristic of Cammie to not offer some sort of an excuse or justification for her behavior, particularly if she thought it might get her out of a punishment. In their time together, he had learned though she was often stubborn and uncooperative, she was never dishonest. What troubled him now was the fact that his gut told him there was more to her misbehavior than met the eye and yet she seemed unwilling to tell him what that was.

Frankly, it hurt to think she might be withholding something from him. Had he not spent the past week showering her with affection and reassurances of his devotion to her?

He finished his drink and set it upon the desk. Rolling back his sleeves, it was time for punishment to begin.

"I noticed you did not ask about the parcel which I purchased from Mrs. Stilton. Are you not curious?"

"Yes, Papa, I am curious." Cammie's voice was soft and distant as she spoke against the sofa's arm. "But I was already in so much trouble I felt I should not ask any questions and to wait patiently because you would tell me when it was appropriate."

"Oh, so now you are willing to wait patiently?"

"I am sorry, Papa." Her sniffles made his heart squeeze again, but he had a task to complete.

"Well, let me show you what I purchased." He unwrapped the brown paper and opened up the box which contained a series of butt plugs which he had ordered to train the little pucker of his new wife. He had already been exploring her tight bottom hole with his fingers and looked forward to the day when he would plunder her there with his cock. However her training needed to commence immediately in order for that to happen.

He placed the smallest of the plugs in the palm of his hand, walked over to his wife and held it in front of her face so she could see. "This, my dear wife, is a training plug which I am going to insert into your bottom hole." Her face blanched and her eyes grew wide as she turned to look at him then glanced back at the piece in his hand and back up at him.

"Papa, it's so big." Her brows knitted together and her bottom lip quivered.

"Camellia, I am losing patience with you. Has not the issue between us all day been your lack of trust in my judgment? I instructed you to stay in your seat at Mrs. Stilton's and you did not. You made a decision that you knew better and you wandered around the shop by yourself. What is worse, you disrespected my wishes."

"I know I did, Papa, and I apologize. I'm so very, very sorry for not heeding your instructions, but..." And then she clamped her mouth shut and said no more. He had no idea what could have transpired in those few minutes that she was alone with the shopgirl at Mrs. Stilton's. Nothing was broken or missing, no injuries. She simply was not where she had been told to remain. Her determination to keep her reasons to herself troubled him most.

It seemed the purchase of butt plugs could not have happened at a more opportune time.

He took the few steps back to where his wife had her butt angled over the arm of the sofa, both of her hands dug deep into the cheeks of her bottom and holding it open for his inspection. "You have such a pretty bunghole, Cammie. Did you know that?"

"Oh, Papa! Please, it is too shameful to discuss such things."

~

CAMMIE HAD NEVER HEARD of a butt plug, though its meaning seemed pretty self-evident to her. Which meant that soon her little bottom was going to be filled with the object which Papa had held in his palm.

She had been shocked to find out that Mrs. Stilton sold naughty items in her store which was otherwise filled with such beautiful goods. Who would have imagined that behind the colorful displays of hats, gloves and handkerchiefs, Mrs. Stilton purveyed erotic toys. Did Priscilla know?

Just thinking about her new acquaintance reminded Cammie of her brother, Robert, and the fact that, in just three days, she had to figure out a way to get herself back to the hat shop in order to meet up with him.

She knew that her papa wanted an explanation from her for why she left her seat, but she simply did not dare to tell him. She hated keeping a secret from Papa, but she hated even more the idea of what his reaction might be to finding out that her brother was nearby. Would Papa tell her she couldn't see Robert? That she was his wife and could not be associating with delivery boys and shopgirls?

Oh, her thoughts perked up. If Robert and Priscilla married, she would get a sister. What a happy notion.

Would Robert be pleased to see her? Or was he glad to have been rid of her for all this time so that he could go on with his own life? Was he happy? Did he have enough to eat and a roof over his head? She was glad to know he had a job and even happier that there seemed to be someone in his life who cared about him. But she still had her doubts about how Papa would feel at the prospect of welcoming members of Cammie's lowborn family into Ashton Manor.

She hated that she had disappointed Papa and she hated even more that she was about to get her bottom punished with a butt plug. She pressed her face against the fabric of the sofa and continued to hold her bottom cheeks apart in the shameful way Papa had instructed her to.

She could feel Papa's breath as he leaned down to inspect

her private hole. 'Twas shameful to have him so close to her naughty parts but she knew this was just the beginning. She squirmed as cool liquid slid down the crack between her cheeks. Next she felt the pressure of the hard plug tapping against her bottom hole.

"Relax, Cammie." Papa's voice interrupted her thoughts. "It will go in if you'll just relax and loosen up the muscles here in your bunghole."

"Oh, Papa. I am so sorry. A million times sorry. Must we do this?" She did not know when she had ever felt so miserable.

"If it makes you feel any better, Cammie, I had planned to purchase the plugs on our trip to the shop today. The only difference is that I intend to use them now to prove a point about obedience. The same point I intended to make when we left the shop without any hats at all. Hats are for good girls who behave themselves when they go shopping. Butt plugs are for naughty girls who disobey. Which girl were you today, Cammie?"

"I-I was a naughty girl, Papa." She sniffled into the sofa.

"You most certainly were. Now keep your cheeks spread wide apart while I finish. Just a little further and this plug will be snug in your pucker."

Cammie did her best to relax, just as she had done the times when Papa had probed her bottom hole with his fingers. She took a deep breath and willed the ring of muscles at the opening of her hole to loosen up so Papa could press the plug further into her. With a little bit of concentration, she managed to relax and she felt the hard object breach the opening to her bottom and work its way past that tight ring of muscles.

Despite the humiliating circumstances, a soft moan of pleasure escaped her lips. She truly was the worst sort of trollop to enjoy such activities. It made her all the more convinced that her mother must have been a prostitute. She wondered if she would be able to ask Robert about that when she saw him on Friday. Or perhaps it was not the type of question she ought to ask first thing.

Papa continued to work the plug in and out and round and round making sure it was properly seated in her bottom. Cammie suspected he enjoyed watching her squirm as he maneuvered the intruder around her bottom.

"Good girl, Cammie," Papa said. "You may put your hands down. You did an excellent job of keeping your bottom cheeks open for Papa."

He gave her bottom three quick swats on each cheek, which caused her to contract her muscles and clench the plug even tighter inside her bottom hole.

"The plug is not always meant as punishment, Cammie. I plan for you to enjoy having my cock deep inside your bottom, when the time comes." He gave the plug a tap and gentle twist and despite her misery at being punished and disappointing Papa, a wave of desire moved through Cammie and she rubbed her lady parts against the arm of the sofa.

"Today, however, the plug will serve a dual purpose of training your hole and reminding you who you belong to, who is the master of your body."

"You are, Papa." Her heart ached with love for him, even though her current situation filled her with shame and dread. Her papa wanted to take care of her and she wanted to give him herself, body and soul.

She really ought to tell him about Robert. Resolved, she opened her mouth to speak, but snapped it shut when Papa took hold of her hand and pulled it down to her bottom and placed her fingers over the plug in her bum. "Do you feel that, Cammie? I put a plug in your back hole because it is mine, mine to do with as I please. Is that correct?"

Shame filled but fascinated, Cammie's fingertips stroked around the end of the plug. "Y-yes, Papa." Her fingers lingered on the very end of the plug, where it felt as though it was engraved.

Papa, observing her closely, of course, noticed. "Those are my initials, Cammie. My mark of ownership. Lest you forget that you belong to me."

CHAPTER 12

Cammie stood outside Mrs. Stilton's millinery shop, her heart pounding, her face flush with exhilaration. She had managed, somehow, to make it on foot from Ashton Manor all the way to Mrs. Stilton's shop only having to ask directions once. She could not believe her good fortune that day, luck had certainly been on her side and she hoped it meant the rest of her plan would go well so that she could speak with Robert and still make it back to Ashton Manor before anyone, particularly Papa, noticed she was missing.

She had woken full of excitement and trepidation. It was Friday, the day she would be able to meet up with Robert, her long lost brother, at Mrs. Stilton's hat shop—if only she could get there in time. She still had not told her papa about her brother. She screwed up her courage thinking she would have to tell Papa the truth in order to persuade him to take her to the hat shop, unless she could convince him to take her to the millinery shop without disclosing the real purpose of her mission there.

Eventually Papa would have to find out. She could not leave the shop again or wander in the alley chatting with a delivery man without Papa finding out and he would not be pleased.

However, serendipity had shown upon Cammie that morning when she had been standing upon the dressing stool while Papa put the finishing touches on her morning apparel. It was a pretty yellow dress which she had long admired while it was hanging in her closet. But she had not had the nerve to ask Papa for permission to wear it since he took such pleasure in selecting her clothing for her each day himself.

Though she was excited to think she would look her very best when she got to finally see her brother after all these years, anxiety roiled through her tummy. Would Robert be angry? Would he recognize her? Would he be pleased to see her or worst of all—what if she was wrong and it was not her brother and she simply made a fool of herself, and risked Papa's ire, all for nothing?

"Papa," she had said hesitantly. "I have been a very good girl for the last three days, have I not?" Of course, she meant the time since the wretched incident the last time they were at Mrs. Stilton's shop and she prayed Papa would not bring that up again.

"As a matter of fact, Cammie, you have. I'm very proud of you. You have done an outstanding job with your bottom hole training and I am very proud of you. I also think you've learned your lesson from the trouble at the millinery shop earlier this week, do you not agree?"

A weight lifted from Cammie's shoulders. "Yes, Papa. And that is what I wish to discuss with you." She wrung her hands together and screwed up her courage. "Do you think, Papa, that perhaps today, if I promise to be a very, very good girl, we could return to Mrs. Stilton's hat shop?"

Papa looked at her and paused. She held her breath and her heart pounded in her chest. "As a matter of fact, my dear,

I think that is a lovely idea. You have been a very good girl and I do not want you to think that I hold a grudge. As I've told you many times, once your punishment is complete, the deed is forgotten and you have earned yourself another trip to see the wares at Mrs. Stilton's shop."

A huge smile of relief flashed across Cammie's face and she practically jumped up and down on the stool. "Oh, Papa, thank you, thank you, thank you," she said. "I promise that I will be a very, very good girl while we are gone."

"I have no doubts, little Cammie. Now, shall we go to breakfast? You will need your strength if you are to go shopping."

Papa assisted Cammie down from the dressing stool by wrapping his large hands around her waist, lifting her in the air and swinging her around the room before setting her feet upon the floor. "Papa," she said, "You are in a happy mood today."

"I am. I'm going to take my wife shopping." He tucked her hand into the crook of his arm and escorted her to the breakfast room.

Over breakfast Cammie laid her plan for how she would sneak away or get a message to Robert. Perhaps she would simply write a note and ask Priscilla to give it to him. That would be the easiest way and Papa would be less likely to find out. Plus, it would be a good back up plan in case she and Robert were not there at the same time. She could not keep asking Papa to take her hat shopping. She just had to hope Robert would get her message and get in touch with her. She congratulated herself on a wise course of action that would achieve her goal and also, hopefully, protect her bottom.

However, her plan changed again when the butler entered the breakfast room. "Pardon me, Lord Cavendish," he said. "But an express has just arrived for you and it appears it is quite urgent. I'm sorry to disturb your breakfast, but I assumed you would like to see this right away."

Papa collected the letter from the tray on which it rested, opened it and quickly read the contents. His brows knitted with worry as he read, and Cammie wondered what it might be about. To her credit, however, she kept her tongue and did not ask. Papa would share with her what she needed to know, nothing more, nothing less.

Papa folded the letter and put it back on the tray before speaking to Cammie. "My apologies, my dear, I am going to have to cancel our outing today. There is an issue which requires my immediate attention, and I will be spending the better part of the day with my solicitor."

"Oh no, Papa. I hope that nothing is wrong," Cammie said, her mind spinning with this change in plans.

"Nothing for you to be concerned about. My only regret is that we will not be able to spend the day together. However, I expect to be home by dinner time and I will look forward to seeing you then. I apologize that we will not be able to go to back to Mrs. Stilton's shop today, but I promise that when we go tomorrow, I will buy you an extra special present to make up for it. How would that be?"

A whole day to herself to get to the milliner's shop and pass her message to Priscilla. Cammie worked hard not to show her excitement. Even with the promise of a special present, Papa would be hurt if she did not appear disappointed at missing out on a day with him. All she really cared about was getting to the millinery today. Nonetheless, she gave Papa a sad smile and said, "Of course, Papa. I will miss you."

As Papa left the room, he looked at her. "Now, Cammie, you are not to leave this house without my permission. And since I will not be here to give permission, that means you are not to leave this house at all. There is plenty for you to do to keep you occupied and out of trouble. You have toys, games and books in your bedroom. It would not hurt for you to practice on the piano, either. I am sure you do not need me to remind you how disappointed I will be if you do not follow my directions."

Cammie's bottom clenched up in response to the implications of Papa's words. "Oh, I do not need a reminder, Papa. I am well aware. You have a good day and I hope everything goes well with the solicitor. I will see you at dinner time."

Papa leaned down and placed a kiss upon her forehead before leaving the room.

Cammie pushed the food around on her breakfast plate until she was certain Papa's carriage had left. Then she hurried from the breakfast room up to her bedroom where she collected a few things for her journey and also made a hasty stop in Papa's library where she found paper and a quill and wrote a note for Robert in case she was not able to speak to him directly.

While seated at Papa's desk, she had remembered the money he kept in one of the drawers. She had a beautiful home and servants and her dear brother had to work as a delivery man. Surely it would not be too wrong to try to assist him, would it?

And now she stood upon the sidewalk in the morning sun nervously waiting for the delivery wagon operated by her brother, Robert.

She tapped her foot and tried not to notice the passersby who glanced curiously at her standing alone in front of Mrs. Stilton's millinery. Peeking through the shop window, she noticed Priscilla and gave a slight wave. The shopgirl hurried out the front door.

"Lady Cavendish," she said, "will you not come into the store? You ought not to be out here alone, especially not in the heat of the day."

Cammie smiled at the young lady. "Has Robert the delivery man arrived yet?" she asked.

Priscilla pulled back and gaped at her. "I beg your pardon, Lady Cavendish, but why is he of interest to you? Are you expecting some particular wares?"

"N-no," Cammie said, realizing she had spoken too soon and had made Priscilla suspicious. "I am simply curious about him."

"Why would a lady like you be curious about a delivery man?" Priscilla put her hands on her hips, appraising Cammie skeptically. "I knew something did not seem proper about you. Is it not enough for you to be married to Lord Cavendish, you must also seek the attention of my beau?"

"No, it is not what you think." Cammie reached into her bag and pulled out the letter addressed to Robert as well as a handful of banknotes which she waved at Priscilla. "Please, give these to him."

Priscilla's mouth hung open. "I will do no such thing. How dare you? Do you think because you are rich you can purchase anything...or anyone...you wish?"

"Please," Cammie said. "I have explained it all in this letter."

"Get away from me." Priscilla turned to go back to her job. Desperate, Cammie grabbed her hand and pressed the bills and letter into it, but Priscilla kept her fingers clenched in a fist.

"You there," a deep voice accosted her, followed by a firm hand on her upper arm. "What are you about?"

"Robert, she was asking after you. What is the meaning of this? Who is she to you?" Priscilla was practically in hysterics, angry tears glistened in the corners of her eyes.

"Priscilla," he said, ignoring Cammie but not loosening his grip on her arm, "I have no idea what you are talking about." He gave Cammie a cursory glance before turning back to Priscilla. "I have never seen this woman before in my life."

"Priscilla! What on earth are you doing? And causing a scene in front of my shop no less. Oh my heavens. Lady Cavendish, is that you? Unhand her." Mrs. Stilton exited her store and charged at Robert, wrapping both her hands around his so that Cammie now had two people and three hands tussling over her right arm.

"Please," she said, "I can explain."

~

ALEXANDER PEEKED out the carriage window, relieved that Ashton Manor was finally in sight. He had spent the morning meeting with his solicitor and he was glad to be returning home earlier than expected. The matter had not been nearly as dire as his solicitor had made it out to be and Alexander had explained quite succinctly his displeasure at having his plans disrupted. However, he was pleased that the whole day had not been wasted. He had told Cammie not to expect him until shortly before dinner, and he couldn't wait to see her face when he surprised her.

He glanced at the wrapped package in his hands, which contained some brand new sheet music for her to try on the piano. Once he'd learned Cammie knew how to play, he'd had his mother's old piano tuned and brought into the drawing room. His little bride had put on several performances for him in the proceeding days, sometimes even singing along as she played.

He smiled to himself. Since her arrival, she'd filled Ashton Manor with an abundance of joy and light. His whole life had changed the moment she'd walked into it, and for the better. He couldn't recall having ever felt so happy and complete. His breath caught. Cammie was the other half of his soul.

God, he loved her. He told her so every day and took pleasure in the slight flush that always stained her cheeks when she demurely said she loved him in return.

The carriage pulled to a stop, and Alexander exited before his footman had a chance to open the door. He was too excited to see Cammie and give her the present. His footman stood awkwardly beside the carriage, giving him a strange look, as Alexander rushed up the steps of his home.

But Cammie was nowhere to be found. She wasn't in the drawing room. Nor was she in her bedroom, or his bedroom. Alexander called out her name as he rushed around the house, only for his butler to approach him with a worried expression.

"I'm afraid I haven't seen her since breakfast, my lord. None of the servants have. She appears to be…missing."

Missing? No, she couldn't be. Where would she have gone? He'd told her that she wasn't to leave the premises of Ashton Manor by herself without permission. He searched the gardens one last time. Still no sign of her. Frowning, he stormed through the house, calling her name, as he approached his library. Since she had plenty of books in her room, she never tended to venture there unless he invited her, and he had forbidden her from touching his desk. But perhaps she had disobeyed and was now hiding there, not daring to come out because she didn't want a spanking.

He burst into his library and scanned the spacious room.

"Cammie! If you keep hiding from me, I promise your punishment will be much worse than I'm already planning." He approached his desk, noting the contents on the top were out of place. His quill and ink were shifted to the left, and a stack of correspondence had been toppled over. He didn't have a direct view of the area behind his desk, and he surmised she must be hiding there.

"Cammie, I am quickly losing my patience. I'm going to

count to three, little girl, and if you don't come out from your hiding place, I will take a strap to you."

He heard no movement, not even a catch of her breath. Very well. He would start counting. It angered him that the first time he'd left her alone, she'd misbehaved and not only entered his library, but had disturbed the contents on his desk and continued hiding from him. Another step forward, and he noticed one of the top drawers had been opened as well, fueling his anger even further. He was a man of order and conducted much of his business from his library. It wasn't a playroom and Cammie had a lot of explaining to do.

"One…two…three." He cleared his throat. "Very well, then. I will fetch you myself, and I doubt once I'm through with you that you'll be sitting comfortably for quite some time."

He strode for his large mahogany desk and rounded it, only to discover Cammie wasn't hiding there as he'd suspected. A cold hand of worry clutched his heart. Several of the desk drawers were opened, including the one where he kept coins and banknotes. He gathered the scattered notes and thumbed through the stack. Some of the money was missing. Not a huge amount, but enough that he would have noticed, even if his desk would have been left in pristine condition.

His worry deepened. Cammie was missing, and someone had stolen from him.

Though he trusted his staff, many of whom had served his family since before his parents' passing, he kept the drawer locked and the key hidden behind a small painting in his library. However, he'd retrieved the key in question once while Cammie had been in his company.

His heart ached from the evidence of his little wife's betrayal. Had she stolen from him and run off? He replayed their last few interactions in his mind, for some indication that she'd been planning this, or any hints that she'd been unhappy in their marriage. She'd been rather quiet during breakfast, now that he thought about it. He also still had a nagging suspicion that she hadn't been honest with him about what had happened at the millinery shop when she'd disobeyed him and knocked over the gloves. This additional thought troubled him further in this moment, though he still couldn't gather why she'd jumped out of her seat and run across the shop without any warning, or what it had to do with her sudden disappearance and thievery.

"Oh, Cammie," he whispered, his voice raspy with grief. "Oh, Cammie, what have you done?"

Alexander looked up from his desk and saw his butler standing in the doorway.

"Lord Cavendish, would you like the carriage readied?" The man pressed his lips together in a show of decorum. At least the servant had the tact not to say, "Would you like a carriage readied so you can hunt down your missing, thieving wife?"

"Yes. Right away." Alexander found the key beneath his chair. Cammie must have left in a hurry. Had she returned to Talcott House? Or...had she decided to go shopping?

He thought of their recent trip to the millinery shop, and the punishment which had followed. Although she had accepted his discipline and the butt plug without too much fuss, and she had behaved perfectly ever since, he had indeed sensed she was holding something back from him. He had to believe that whatever secret she was keeping related to her disappearance as well as the missing money. But even with those clues he was flummoxed at trying to decipher her motive or plan. He doubted she'd taken the money to get herself a hat. She had many new hats in her sizeable closet, most of which she hadn't even worn yet. Besides that, she had never shown a predisposition for material things. She always seemed overwhelmingly grateful for every little comfort or bobble he gave her. God, where had she gone?

Her disappearance gutted him.

He left the package that contained the music sheets on his messy desk and bounded outside for the carriage.

"To Talcott House," he told the driver. "As fast as possible."

"Of course, my lord," the driver said, climbing up to his seat. Alexander entered the carriage, the footman closing the door behind him seconds before the wheels started rolling.

The hat shop was on the way to Talcott House. On the slim chance she'd gone shopping, perhaps he would spot her in the street. She had seemed to make a connection with the shopgirl there. Perhaps she had needed some companionship with a girl near her own age, though Alexander would prefer it to be the wife or daughter of one of his neighbors rather than a common shopgirl. He chided himself for being remiss in introducing her to ladies of her own station. He had been selfish in keeping her to himself.

Of course, her running off to Talcott House didn't make sense either. They were man and wife. She belonged to him. Didn't she realize he would track her to the very ends of the Earth? And if she truly meant to elude him, surely she must know that would be the first place he looked.

Anxiety knotted in his stomach. He gazed out the carriage windows, moving right and left between each of the two sides of the street, desperate to find her. He had dressed her in a yellow gown that morning. He looked for a flash of yellow and hoped she hadn't changed before leaving Ashton Manor. Changing clothes by herself was also strictly against his rules, but given current events, he supposed he wouldn't be surprised to find her wearing a different dress. But still, he had yet to spot a slight feminine figure that resembled his little Cammie, and as the minutes ticked by and the carriage barreled through the streets, his apprehension grew.

What if something bad had happened to her after she ran off? Dire possibilities swirled through his head. *Please God, let me find her. Let me find her unharmed.* She'd lived a sheltered life in Talcott House and had obviously left his estate on foot. What if she had ventured into a disreputable part of town? He couldn't bear the thought of any harm coming to his sweet little girl, and when he finally found her he would...he would *what*?

Cold fear gripped him. Maybe she'd had a change of heart.

What if she'd run off because she didn't want to be his little girl anymore?

No, he told himself. No, that couldn't be the reason she was gone. There had to be another explanation. Yet he couldn't come up with a reason for the missing money and her absence that made any more sense than her having had a change of heart.

"Stop!" he shouted, banging on the carriage roof.

There she was. Standing near the hat stop, in her yellow dress, her matching yellow parasol lying on the sidewalk while Mrs. Stilton and a young man he had never seen grappled with his wife's arm and Mrs. Stilton's shopgirl glared at Cammie.

~

ALEXANDER TUMBLED from the carriage before it came to a stop. He hit the sidewalk at a dead run and sent both Mrs. Stilton and the heathen of a man who had dared touch his wife tumbling to the ground when he grabbed Cammie from their grasp.

Tucking Cammie behind him protectively, he squared his shoulders and put up his fists. From the corner of his eye he could see that a crowd of curious onlookers had gathered.

This was hardly the behavior expected of a gentleman of his status, but where his wife's safety was at issue, he cared not for public opinion and prepared to defend her, with his own life if necessary.

"Come on," he goaded the other man as he stood up, "let's see if you are as brave when attacking a man as you are about attacking a helpless woman."

"Sir, I assure you I did not attack her, I was simply attempting to prevent her from harming Priscilla," he said, nodding toward the shopgirl.

"Rubbish. What sort of coward blames a woman for his troubles? Get over here and defend yourself." He waved his fists in the air like a crazed pugilist, waiting for the other man to engage in the fight, never letting his guard down.

"My lord." Cammie tugged at the tail of his coat.

"Not now, Cammie," he said, giving her a quick glance. It was enough of a distraction however, for the other man to see an advantage and he took a swing, landing an impressive blow to Alexander's jaw, sending him backward on top of Cammie who had been unable to get out of the way fast enough.

Alexander recovered quickly, though. By this time, the driver and footmen had joined the fracas, forming a perimeter around him while he rubbed his jaw and regained his footing, his fists were in the air again.

"Cammie," he ordered, "get in the carriage and wait for me there." Turning to his servants he said, "See to Lady Cavendish's safety. I shall handle this matter myself."

Tears were streaming down Cammie's face and she clung to his arm. "Cammie," he assured her, "I shall be fine. Please do as I tell you."

"My lord," she implored him, "he is my brother."

It was an odd gathering around the tea table in Mrs. Stilton's parlor. Cammie was overwhelmed with misery over all the trouble she had caused, and dreaded the punishment she knew awaited her upon her return to Ashton Manor. For right now, however, she did not care. Her heart sung at being seated next to her brother.

"Jane, I never would have recognized you," he said. His use of her birth name gave her pause. "You have grown up into a beautiful young woman."

"Thank you." She blushed. His praise meant everything to her. "I am sorry for the confusion I created," she said, looking around the table and making eye contact with each person, including Papa who sat on her other side. Sandwiched between her brother and her husband, Cammie felt whole and complete, utterly content.

"I am sorry for being suspicious of you," Priscilla said. "I could not imagine any reason why Lady Cavendish would be curious about Robert." Her loving gaze landed on Cammie's brother.

"It would seem," Papa finally spoke, "that both Robert and I are very protective of the women we love. It can cause a man to act impulsively. I hope you will accept my apology as well." He held his palm out to Robert and the two men clasped hands in front of Cammie.

Her heart filled with love for the two most important men in her life.

However, she also knew that although everything had ended well with her plan to find Robert, her Papa would not be satisfied with a handshake from her.

CHAPTER 13

Cammie stood, naked and ashamed, in the corner of Papa's library, trembling and filled with more regret than she'd ever known. What had she been thinking? Papa was so angry with her. She'd broken his trust. Would he ever forgive her?

Tears rolled down her cheeks and she sniffled. Behind her, she heard papers being shuffled and drawers being closed. She'd been in such a hurry to leave and find Robert that she hadn't taken time to clean up the mess she'd made, and now Papa was straightening up after her carelessness. He hadn't said much during the carriage ride home, but she'd felt the anger radiating off him. She was so upset over having disappointed him that she almost didn't care how he punished her. But his next words made her blood run cold.

"You will receive a spanking followed by a dose of the strap."

"Papa?" she asked tearfully, not daring to turn around yet. He hadn't given her permission to move.

"You know what you did wrong, young lady. We promised to be honest with one another, but you failed to tell me you saw your brother last week in the hat shop. Then you plotted to leave the manor in secret, to meet your brother after years apart and not even knowing what kind of man he'd turned into. He could have hurt you. Or you could have run into trouble on the street. God, Cammie, you could have been robbed or worse. Did it not occur to you how close you might have been to a tragic ending?"

A sob built in her throat and she trembled harder. He was right. She had been secretive and impulsive and put herself in danger, not to mention worried her Papa. She hadn't expected him to come home early today and couldn't imagine what he'd initially thought when he discovered she'd stolen from him and run off.

"I'm so sorry, Papa," she said, forcing the words out. Her throat burned so fiercely with emotion that each syllable was a challenge. "And I'm sorry for stealing from you."

"Christ, Cammie. I don't care about the money. What is mine is yours." He grabbed her and spun her around, out of the corner. His face was etched in lines of fury, her brows drawn together and his jaw clenched. "Are you allowed to leave this house without permission?"

"No, Papa."

"Are you allowed to keep secrets from me?"

Her lips quivered. "No-no, Papa."

"Are you allowed to put yourself in danger?" His eyes blazed, his nostrils flared, and he tightened his hold on her shoulders.

She parted her lips and tried to answer, but her voice failed her. She buried her face in her hands and burst into tears. She wept for her mistakes. She wept for all the years she'd wondered about Robert's fate and her relief that he wasn't still living on the streets. But most of all, she wept for how badly she had scared her Papa and caused him to worry about her. He was correct, of course. Venturing off by herself in London had been stupid. She'd gotten lost once and had to ask for directions. Luckily, the two passersby had been kind and helpful, pointing her down the right street. But Papa had spent over an hour in a state of panic as he searched for her.

A horrible thought suddenly struck her. She uncovered her face and peered at him.

"I hope you didn't think I was leaving you, Papa! Oh, I would never do such a thing!"

He tensed, but some of the anger left his eyes. "I won't lie to you. The thought crossed my mind, Cammie, though I found myself at a loss for a reason. You-you are happy living here and being my wife and my little girl, are you not?"

"I'm very happy here with you, Papa. I swear it. I love you with all my heart. I would never leave you, and I'm so sorry for everything today. I-I know broke a lot of important rules and I deserve the harshest punishment."

He loosened his grip on her shoulders and his expression relaxed. She knew he was still displeased with her, but the scary angry look had dispersed from his gaze.

"I love you too, Cammie, and that is why I must ensure you never put yourself in danger again. That is the worst rule you could ever break. If something happened to you, I…I can't even bear the thought of it. You are my world, little girl." He cupped the side of her face.

She leaned into his touch, soaking up his affection. She resolved to follow his orders during her punishment and not beg for leniency, no matter how much it hurt. A tingle raced across her bottom and her cheeks clenched, but the desire she often felt while Papa scolded her or threatened chastisement was absent. The situation was too grave, and she was simply too distraught over her actions to feel anything but a deep desperation to mend the rift between them.

All she wanted was for Papa to smile at her again. To hold her and tell her she was his good girl. More tears spilled over and she sniffled for the umpteenth time. She glanced around his library, noting that he'd set everything back to rights. Papa liked to keep things in perfect order.

He dropped his hand from her face and led her toward his desk. He'd laid her dress and underthings over a nearby chair, and she gave a mournful glance at the garments, wishing she weren't entirely naked. She'd never been punished over Papa's big grown up desk before, and the formality of being led, while not wearing a stitch of clothing, to his desk where a leather strap rested, made her tummy flutter with fresh nerves.

"Over the desk, young lady." He brought her in front of the desk and guided her to bend down.

She placed her hands on the hard surface, following his direction. He stepped back and she felt his eyes on her. She heard him walk away and wondered what he was doing, but he soon returned and lifted her high enough to place a pillow he'd taken from the sofa between her stomach and the desk. His kindness—that he would endeavor to ensure her comfort even while he thrashed her—made her feel all the worse for the worry she'd caused him.

"I've scolded you enough," he said quietly. "I believe you understand what you've done wrong, and I know that you are sorry for it, but I'm afraid I still cannot go easy on you during this punishment, Cammie." He paused for a moment, as if waiting for his words to sink in. "I hope that I never have to punish you this severely again, and it is my hope that you'll think twice before you behave in such an impulsive manner again."

He stood close to her and placed a steadying hand on her lower back. She resisted the urge to clench her cheeks. Closing her eyes, she prayed for the strength to not make a fool of herself and beg him to go easy on her.

He gave her bottom a squeeze and a second later cracked his palm across her flesh.

She gasped but remained still, with her bottom raised up to accept each searing smack he gave her. He continued on for some time, slapping first her left cheek, then her right one, and even striking the tender tops of her thighs. She started sobbing again, but she didn't ask him to stop, and she certainly didn't ask him to spare the strap.

Fire blazed across her bottom cheeks and upper thighs. She gasped when he applied a series of especially hard swats to the lower curve of her behind. By some miracle, she managed to keep her feet planted on the floor.

Finally, Papa stopped spanking. She opened her eyes to see him reaching for the thick leather strap. Her stomach lurched and panic swelled. She took a few deep breaths, trying to brace herself for the final part of her punishment. Papa loved her, and she trusted him not to cause her any true harm, but was still scared of how badly the strap would hurt. She sniffled, hoping he hugged her after the strapping ended.

"These final twelve will be quick and hard, Cammie." There was an edge of despair to his voice that she didn't quite understand. "Promise you will be honest with me from this day forward. Promise that you will not keep secrets. Papa can't take care of all your needs if you are keeping secrets and sneaking around behind my back, let alone running off into the streets of London unsupervised and without permission. *Promise,* Cammie."

"I-I promise, Papa. No se-secrets ever ag-again," she said through her increasing tears.

He pressed a firm hand to her back. An instant later, she heard the whoosh of the strap and heard it crack over her buttocks before she even felt the pain. But when the pain registered, she cried out, unable to help herself. Oh heavens. How would she endure eleven more?

She pressed her lips together and somehow managed to remain quiet during the next two strokes, both delivered slightly lower than the first lash. She would never sit down again, of that she was certain. She would also be the perfect little girl for Papa from now on. She'd made herself that promise before, but this time she meant it. Seeing the disappointment reflected in her papa's gaze had left her shaken. She'd known she loved him before today, but she hadn't realized the profound depth of that love until she had so seriously disappointed him.

She lost count of the lashes and drifted in the pain wrought from her actions. He brought the leather down again and again. *Whoosh. Crack. Whoosh. Crack.* She gasped and writhed on the desk, and while she lurched up on her tiptoes a few times, her feet never completely left the floor.

She heard a thud and opened her eyes, trying to focus through her tears. Papa had tossed the strap on the floor.

It was over. She'd survived it. But what if her papa was still cross with her? Would he truly forgive her so quickly? She cried harder. He might need a few days to calm down, and she wouldn't blame him at all. What if he made her sleep in her little girl room, bereft of his touch and his comfort? She covered her face, unable to bear the thought of his coldness toward her. She would endure a punishment like this every day of her life, if only he would wrap his arms around her and snuggle her close.

HE'D BEEN HARD on her. He told himself he had no choice, but God, hearing her uncontrollable sobbing wrenched at his heart.

Alexander lifted Cammie off the desk and carried her to the sofa. He sat her on his lap and stroked the tear-matted hair from her face. Her crying finally subsided and when she met his gaze, her eyes widened and she appeared positively panicked.

"It's over now, Cammie. You took your punishment well. I'm very proud of you, and as I said before, I hope I never have cause to be so strict with you again." He smoothed her hair behind her ears and started to worry when she didn't respond. "Cammie?"

"Am-am I forgiven, Papa?" she asked in a shaky whisper.

"God, yes. Of course you are forgiven. Is that why you looked so upset, little girl? You were worried Papa wasn't going to forgive you?"

"I was so naughty, I worried you might need a few days before you weren't angry with me anymore. And I-I worried you wouldn't hold me…afterward," she confessed as silent tears trickled down her cheek.

He caught a tear with his thumb and leaned in to kiss her forehead. "You are forgiven, Cammie. You were naughty—very much so—but you repented and took your punishment, and now all is forgiven, the slate wiped clean. I'm no longer angry with you, and I will hold you for as long as you need. You're my little girl and I've vowed to always take care of your needs. Even if I was angry with you and you needed a hug, I would never think of withholding affection from you as part of your punishment. Do you understand?" he said gently.

"Oh, Papa. I am so relieved. You really are the best papa in the whole wide world." She threw her arms around him and hugged him tight. "I'm so lucky to have you."

"I'm the lucky one," he replied, snuggling her closer and stroking her hair. He pulled a handkerchief from his pocket and dabbed at her face and nose, tending to her as a good papa should.

He held her until she fell asleep in his arms. Then he

and he increased his pace and gripped her hips, lost in his primal need to claim her. A high-pitched whimper escaped her, and a second later he felt the walls of her cunny clamping down tight on his cock.

"That's it, little Cammie. Come on Papa's cock like a good girl."

Not long after, the first wave of his release hit him, his balls seizing up and his cock exploding as he filled her with his seed, pumping deep into her tightness. He withdrew from her carefully and laid down beside her, pulling the covers overtop them both and drawing her close, folding her snugly into his embrace. She gave a sigh of deep contentment and her breaths tickled his chest. His heart swelled to bursting, he was so overcome with affection for her. Indeed, little Cammie was the other half of his soul.

"I love you so much, Papa." She ran her hands over his back and tangled her legs with his under the covers.

"I love you, too, my sweet little bride. Always and forever."

EPILOGUE

Tonight was the night. She was certain of it.

Cammie paced nervously in Papa's bedroom. He'd ordered her upstairs, telling her to await his arrival in his room, rather than her little girl room. Given all the extra attention he'd shown her bottom hole lately, and given that she'd successfully taken the largest of the plugs the last two days in a row, she suspected he meant to stick his big hard cock into her hiney hole tonight.

She gulped. Papa's manhood was still larger than the biggest plug. Would she be able to take it? Her breath caught in her throat. Would he come inside her back *there*?

Well, she supposed she would find out soon. The telltale sound of his footsteps coming down the hallway made her tummy flip, and she instinctively reached behind herself to shield her bottom, even though Papa wasn't yet in the bedroom. Feeling silly, she forced her arms to her sides and watched the door, her anticipation growing by the second.

His words from weeks ago came rushing back.

All your holes belong to your papa. Your cunny. Your mouth.

And even your rosebud. Whichever hole I want to fill, that's the hole you will take my cock in, little girl.

Papa entered and closed the door behind him. She peered at him, undone by a sudden bout of shyness, despite the fact that they'd been married for a while now. His strong presence dominated the room, and she felt a tad faint as he approached her. Her gaze drifted lower, and she gasped at the sight of his hugeness tenting the front of his trousers.

Papa was already hard for her.

Though she'd come to him an innocent virgin, she now understood that her papa's cock became hard when he desired her. A deep ache pulsed between her thighs, and she hoped he still gave her kitty some attention tonight. Often when he pushed a plug into her bottom hole, he would stroke her privates and circle her sensitive nubbin until she became delirious with the pleasure of it and rode the waves of ecstasy to a mind-numbingly blissful release.

Oh dear. She was certain her drawers were soaking now, her musings had turned so naughty and her privates wouldn't cease clenching and tingling. Her behind cheeks clenched when Papa strode toward her.

"I think you know what's going to happen tonight, don't you, little girl?"

"I-I believe so, Papa."

"Tell me. I want to hear you say it." Lust blazed in his eyes.

"You're going to claim my bottom hole with your manhood, Papa." She gulped and fidgeted in place, twisting her fingers together.

He guided her closer to the bed. "That's correct, little girl. Tonight, that tight pucker between your bottom cheeks is all mine." He stepped behind her and began unfastening the laces on the back of her dress. She trembled as he undressed her, but her shaking wasn't from fright. She was quivering with the anticipation of feeling his hugeness inside the most private part of her. In a way, it felt more intimate than accepting his cock into her cunny. Her breaths quickened and her pulse raced, her heart pounding in her ears.

He pushed her dress down off her shoulders and over her hips, and she stepped out of the garment with his assistance. Next, he stripped off her chemise, stockings, and drawers, leaving her completely bared. It was summer now, and the night was warm enough that a window had been opened, and a light breeze entered to caress her flesh and heighten her senses.

"Get on the bed, little Cammie. Get on your hands and knees for Papa."

She obeyed, crawling atop the covers and getting into position. She lifted her bottom high in the air and arched her back, offering up her bottom to her papa. His breath caught and she smiled to herself, knowing that he must've noticed the moisture coating her bare quim. As she'd moved into position, she'd felt the slickness of it rubbing between her thighs.

"So wet, little girl. It's a shame Papa isn't fucking your cunny tonight."

"Papa! That's bad language."

She heard the telltale sounds of him removing his clothing, and moments later he crawled onto the bed behind her. He gave her bottom a sharp slap. "Yes, it is, and I had better not hear you using grown up words like that ever."

"I'm a good girl," she replied in a saucy tone, giving a slight wiggle of her rear. "You've never had to punish me for using bad language before."

"You have a point." He smacked her bottom again.

"Ouch! Why are you spanking me then?"

"Because you have a cheeky tone right now, young lady, and cheeky little girls get spanked in this household."

"Sorry, Papa," she said, in the most demure voice she could muster.

"That's better." He ran his hands along the curve of her back and shifted closer.

She gasped at the feel of his hardness touching her inner thighs. Then he reared back and boldly pulled her bottom cheeks wide apart.

"Are you nervous, Cammie?"

"A little, Papa. You're so big."

He shifted behind her and she heard a bottle being opened. Well, at least he was planning to use the same oil he used to ease the passage of the plugs into her behind hole. She braced herself for the first jolt of cool liquid being applied to her rosebud, but even knowing it was coming didn't keep her from gasping aloud.

Papa gave a dark chuckle. "I love the way your tiny pucker clenches when I touch it."

Her face heated, and she gripped the covers and sucked in a deep breath. He pushed two fingers in and out of her tightness, and she jerked her center against him, unable to keep her hips from undulating. Her nubbin throbbed, and she wished he would stroke her privates, if only for a moment. But he soon replaced his pummeling digits with the tip of his big hard manhood.

"You can take this, Cammie, I know you can. Keep your bottom soft and let Papa inside."

"I-I'll try my best, Papa."

He worked his way into her snug passage with slow thrusts, each one deeper than the last, until finally, his balls slapped against her cunny. She jolted with the realization that he was hilt deep in her ass, and it hadn't hurt one bit. The oil, combined with the plug training, had actually worked to help her accommodate the fullness of Papa's huge length.

"You're such a good girl, Cammie. How does it feel to have your papa's cock driving in and out of your tight little bottom hole?"

"Oh, Papa. It feels...*good*." She could barely talk, she was so overcome with the sensation of having her rosebud filled and stretched. It felt better than the plugs, because Papa's cock was hot and throbbing. She shuddered and clutched the covers harder, deciding it wouldn't be awful if he thrust a bit faster.

As if reading her mind, he increased his pace and spread her cheeks wider, allowing him to drive even deeper. She whimpered and moaned, lost in the euphoria of her building pleasure. With each hard thrust, Papa's balls slammed against her cunny and directly atop her swollen nubbin. *Smack smack smack*. It wasn't long before she cried out her release, writhing against Papa and arching her back even further to take him as deep as possible.

"Cammie," he growled her name.

She thrilled at the feel of his manhood pulsing suddenly, followed by a blast of warmth as he pumped his seed inside her. After a few moments, during which they both attempted to catch their breath, he began to slowly pull out of her tightness. A trickle of his seed rolled down her thigh after he finally withdrew from her bottom hole. He turned her over and stared into her eyes. His next words made her spirit dance.

"Papa's proud of you, Cammie."

~THE END~

ABOUT THE AUTHORS

SUE LYNDON

USA TODAY bestselling author Sue Lyndon writes steamy D/s romance in a variety of genres, from contemporary to historical to fantasy. She's a #1 Amazon bestseller in multiple categories, including BDSM Erotica and Sci-Fi Erotica. But no matter the genre, her heroes are always HOT dominant alpha males. She also writes non-bdsm sci-fi romance under the name Sue Mercury. When she's not busy working on her next book, you'll find her hanging out with her family, watching sci-fi movies, reading, or sneaking chocolate.

Titles by Sue Lyndon:

Sci-Fi, Fantasy, & Dystopian

Kenan's Mate (Kleaxian Warriors, Book 1)
Tavarr's Mate (Kleaxian Warriors, Book 2)
The Seal's Captive Bride
Taken by the Admiral

Punished by the Admiral
Claiming His Human Wife
Owning His Bride
His by Law (Dark Embrace, Book 1)
Saving His Runaway Bride (Dark Embrace, Book 2)
Claiming Their Maiden (Barbarian Mates, Book 1)
Claiming Their Princess (Barbarian Mates, Book 2)
Claiming Their Slave (Barbarian Mates, Book 3)
Big Blue Valentine
Taming Princess Anna
Surrender (Alien Warriors, Book 1)
Commander's Slave (Alien Warriors, Book 2)
Daman's Ward (Jackson Settlement, Book 1)
Shana's Guardian (Jackson Settlement, Book 2)
Rules of War (Rules of War, Book 1)
Rules of Command (Rules of War, Book 2)

Historical

Sold into Marriage
His Sweet Amber
Conquering Lady Claire
His to Educate
Marriage of Convenience
A Firm Husband (Wyoming Heat, Book 1)
A Strict Husband (Wyoming Heat, Book 2)

Contemporary

Black Light: Roulette Redux
Punished by the Cowboy
His Loving Guidance
Her Old-Fashioned Doctor
His Naughty Valentine

Confessions of a Spanking Author
Maid to Submit
Marry me in Montana
Mine by Christmas
Report for Punishment
It Takes a Dom
Breaking His Rules
Christmas with the Professor
Snowed in with Santa
Tessa's Submission
Valentine Submission
Dark Without You
Mountain Devil

Age play

A Daddy for Christmas
The Girl, the Doctor, and the Texas Ranger
Becoming Little Lexie
His Naughty Little Mate
Hanna's Awakening

Titles by Sue Lyndon writing as Sue Mercury:

Step Alien (Reestrian Mates, Book 1)
Sweet Alien (Reestrian Mates, Book 2)
Double Alien (Reestrian Mates, Book 3)
Boss Alien (Reestrian Mates, Book 4)
Savage Alien (Reestrian Mates, Book 5)
Reestrian Mates: The Complete Series

Alien's Innocent Bride (Mail Order Human, Book 1)
Alien's Princess Bride (Mail Order Human, Book 2)
Alien's Reluctant Bride (Mail Order Human, Book 3)

Alien's Orphan Bride (Mail Order Human, Book 4)
Alien's Beloved Bride (Mail Order Human, Book 5)
Mail Order Human: The Complete Series

Learn more at:

WWW.SUELYNDON.COM

CELESTE JONES

USA Today bestselling author Celeste Jones is known for writing highly entertaining erotic romance featuring headstrong heroines and stern yet loving heroes who aren't afraid to take a naughty woman over their knees. When she's not writing, she enjoys travel, reading and dancing like no one is watching.

Titles by Celeste Jones:

Historical

His Tempestuous Bride (Regency Matchmaker, Book 1)
His Mischievous Bride (Regency Matchmaker, Book 2)
Lady Katherine's Comeuppance (Lady Katherine's Comeuppance, Book 1)
Lady Katherine's Conundrum (Lady Katherine's Comeuppance, Book 2)
Corrected by the Colonel
Maid for a Lord
Willful Miss Winchester
Becoming Lady Amherst

Contemporary

Laying Down the Law
An Old-Fashioned Man
Back to Her Future
Lolly and the Professor
Her Birthday Spanking

Learn more at:

HTTPS://WRITERCELESTEJONES.BLOGSPOT.COM

22727257R00089

Made in the USA
Columbia, SC
05 August 2018